What the Tree Saw

What the Tree Saw

Short Fictions

Peter Biles

RESOURCE *Publications* · Eugene, Oregon

WHAT THE TREE SAW
Short Fictions

Resource Publications
An Imprint of Wipf and Stock Publishers
199 W. 8th Ave., Suite 3
Eugene, OR 97401

www.wipfandstock.com

PAPERBACK ISBN: 979-8-3852-7724-7
HARDCOVER ISBN: 979-8-3852-7725-4
EBOOK ISBN: 979-8-3852-7726-1

VERSION NUMBER 04/29/26

Contents

Part I

Part II

Part III

Part I

Mouse Trap

I.

I bought seven mouse traps yesterday and set them up this morning to give myself some peace of mind.

They're those little round sticky plates that the mice can't escape from. If they try, they break a leg. Otherwise, they starve to death. It sounds awful. I completely realize this and I can't say I'm super comfortable with it. But Faye said these traps were more humane than the ones that get the job done in a nanosecond. I don't know. I just bought them and set them up in the attic, pantry, and the corners of the living room behind the recliner and love seat. I lay awake at night and try to sleep when the little devils scurry up and down the walls like malicious levers designed to thwart domestic peace and quiet. And then I sit straight up in bed and swing my feet over the edge with panache and determination. This, in turn, wakes up Faye, who always says languidly through the wrist over her mouth, "You have to get mouse traps. Not the snappy ones. The *humane* ones."

I've been rapping on the wall to dissuade the critters as if that does anything (it doesn't) and then, perturbed since this is Faye's and my first house together, go into the kitchen to heat up some tea and sit in the recliner to brood and listen to the invasion. Just for once, I'd like to escape *noise.* I'm like the Grinch complaining about all these Whos that populate post-post-modernity: *All the noise, noise, noise, noise!*

Mice are a common problem even in modern America but there are certain inconveniences that at a certain point in one's financial, professional, and relational development one feels entitled to transcend. I have to say that mice infestation is one of those inconveniences. I guess I would've thought that at this point in my life the last thing I'd be worrying about were tiny furry beasts running up and down the architecture of the house, including the attic. And I have a phobia of attics, by the way. Always have. I had half a mind to give an earful to the landlord when I remembered that no, dimwit, *I* am the homeowner now, and that comes with consequences.

Back to the traps, though. I set them out one morning before we went to work (we work in the same firm, both analysts with more or less equal pay depending on monthly commission) and gave it little thought for the whole day. I had deadlines, meetings, market predictions, and the typical sexual tension with Faye to transform into healthy corporate distance. Timmy, the intern fresh out of Yale, tries to make conversation in the break room where we always happen to collide around midmorning. The day of the mouse traps was no different.

"Did you see the game last night?" said Timmy.

"What game?"

Timmy poured coffee on his wrist, missing his mug, and winced. "Uh . . . the baseball game."

"No buddy, I didn't. I was kept awake for most of the night by mice in the walls."

"Really!"

"A fact."

"I'll have to call my uncle. He's an exterminator."

"I think we'll be all right. I set some traps."

"The ones that break their necks or the humane ones?"

I scowled at him, with humor of course, over the rim of my coffee mug and slurped, "Humane ones, *obviously*. Faye wouldn't have it any other way."

Timmy poured himself a new cup, this time with some success, and added, "Well, good. You let me know if they still keep you up at night. I tell you, my uncle is an exterminator. He's good at what he does."

"All right, buddy, thanks."

That afternoon after work, Faye and I took the subway home, talking little, since we use the transport home to shake off our professional identities before resuming our marital selves, walked three blocks to our front yard, and went in with caution. I expected the squeaking of many mice. Instead, a draft of wind blew through a smashed window in the kitchen.

"Oh, God!" shouted Faye. "We've been *hoodwinked*!"

I'm not sure why she opted for the word "hoodwinked," but I chalked it up to shock and strode over to the scene of the crime to investigate. Shattered glass on the floor crinkled under my boots. The drop to the grass outside was about four feet, maybe less. No one stalked the backyard. My new grill still stood on the little raised porch patio. Our spot of natural habitat in the urban jungle looked otherwise undisturbed. Faye meanwhile turned the house upside down in a fell swoop. She pulled on drawers and unlocked our safe. She came back, red-faced but more serene, to let me know that nothing seemed to be missing, not even the necklace she left laying on the dresser.

"Weird," I said.

"Very," she replied. "Um. Well. What do you think did it?"

I put my head through the broken window and glared at the sky. Men tend to make gestures towards their competence even when they don't know what in the Sam hill they're doing.

"No clue. Maybe a baseball?"

"But where's the baseball?"

"I don't know. It wasn't a baseball, then."

Faye checked the house again and returned with the same result.

"Should we stay here tonight?" she said. She put her black hair back in a ponytail and her hands on her hips as I picked up a broom and started to sweep.

"Where would we stay?"

"I don't know. Your sister's, maybe?"

"Yeah, maybe. You're worried about staying here?

"I don't know! What if some creep just came by, bashed the window, saw we were coming, and hopped over the fence before we saw him? What if he comes back to murder us in our sleep and steal everything we own?"

"If we're murdered in our sleep," I chuckled, "we won't care if someone steals everything we own."

"Fine. Joke about it. *I* for one don't really feel super safe."

I threw the glass in the trash bin and remembered the mouse traps.

It was with a weird kind of glee akin to the type I feel when a competing firm gets financially wobbly that I checked the traps. Bit by bit, though, hope turned to gloom. The sticky stuff wasn't messed up at all. None of the traps had even moved an inch. I put my ear against the wall, met silence, and frowned. Faye was packing a duffel in our bedroom.

"Faye, c'mon, I think we're all right."

"I'm going to call your sister."

"I can call the cops maybe?"

"What're you going to tell them? That we got broken into?"

"That someone broke our window, yes."

Maybe (and it's dumb but hear me out) the *mice* broke the window. Teamed up? The glass wasn't military grade after all. Okay, it's stupid. Never mind. Just a thought.

While she packed, I taped a tarp over the open hole and brewed coffee in my Chemex. This always seems to calm me down. Faye came back in and suggested we eat grilled chicken and broccoli for dinner, itching the back of her head, which always seems to calm *her* down. She got out her phone, turned on NPR, and we cooked.

"I guess it isn't too crazy," she said.

"What, the window?"

"Yeah?"

"Yeah. Just weird."

"It was probably a bird, or a pressure thing with the house."

"Yeah. A pressure thing."

We ate on the table on the front porch and watched the occasional person walk past on the walk. It was April, and the days had already gotten a little longer, hinting summer. I sipped the acrid coffee. The sky was a cool blue and garbed with tatters of stratus clouds. I think that means rain. Hopefully the tarp holds. We live on a street with tightly packed houses, each with a tiny yard partitioned by plain white fences, each of which encloses its own square plot of grass that all seem systemically designed to exclude the possibility of neighborly barbecues.

Faye called her mother after dinner; she usually does this in the bathroom, door closed, and that evening was no exception. Meanwhile, I reinforced the tarp and ordered a new window on Amazon. Hope it fits. No way of knowing exactly. The sun was setting now and cast shadows against the kitchen cabinets. Darkness, I knew, meant mice.

All in all, though, we were able to settle down in front of the TV, pour some glasses of wine, and even kiss for a while as evening ripened into night and we started getting ready for bed.

"I'm meeting Sue for coffee in the morning," said Faye.

"Wait. Today's Friday."

"Yes. What'd you think?

"Thursday."

"Nope. It's the weekend, pal!"

She slipped into her bedclothes and crept under the covers.

"That means I can sleep in," I announced. "Which means that if the mice keep us up, we won't be dog tired at work the next morning."

"You're the one who they keep up at night," Faye reminded me.

That was true. I was.

II.

We must've settled down to sleep around ten p.m. It had been a long week for the both of us. A long month, a long year. Faye drifted off after a few minutes, the lucky dog, but I stayed awake and laid on my back with my hands on my chest above the covers. The silence was almost worse than the sounds in the walls. I'm not sure why. Eleven p.m. rolled around. Nothing. Midnight came with a moon smiling through the gathering rain clouds. Not a scratch from our mammalian foes. I turned on my side and tried, honest to God, to fall asleep. The air conditioner kicked on, which helped blot out the oppressive silence, but it only lasted for a couple of minutes, and there I was again, wakeful as ever. I got up to have a look around.

The tarp had held up even with the light patter of rain outside. I turned on the lamp in my study and sat down on the pale leatherwood chair in my robe, naked underneath, with the light of a streetlamp shining through the window. My desk is a picture of sanitation, nothing on it except a book about maximizing life savings and a cup full of pens and pencils. The walls. They were still quiet.

So, why couldn't I sleep?

Maybe I was upset about something. Did Faye say anything to rub me the wrong way? No, I don't think so. Working together has been a little bit weird, of course, but we've been able to separate work from home pretty efficiently. Come to think of it, that's the perfect word to describe our lives. Efficient. It all *works* so well. Life, up to now, has been relatively seamless. College to job to dating to marriage to keeping a friendly distance from our roots. Happily intertwined, we are far away from any kin or old community who might know us as anything else than what we prefer to be seen as, which is, of course, total successes.

I stood up and brewed some tea. The wind ruffled the tarp a little, and drops of rain flecked the other kitchen window. I sipped and relaxed my shoulders. Our house is so clean and new. There isn't a scratch on the walls, no baseboard out of joint, no dried smear of misdirected paint on the ceilings. Just a busted window and mice in the walls. I finished the tea and set the glass cup in the sink. The mice, the one unwelcome aspect of our new house, seem to have left just as the storm arrived.

I crawled back into bed, and right when I was about to go to sleep, the noise in the walls started back up as if responding to an orchestral cue.

What freaked the both of us out wasn't necessarily the scratching itself. No, it was how eerily timed it was with my head hitting the pillow. It was as flawless as clockwork, like the furry little idiots were *waiting* for it.

"That's it," I whispered. Faye rolled over and groaned.

"Again?"

"They're back at it."

It was dumb of me then to think the critters had fled through the window. To the contrary, they were making even more racket tonight.

"What can we *do*?" Faye said as I sat up and swung my feet back over the edge of the bed. I felt the wall, did the usual shtick, fuming all the while.

"I can't do this," said Faye. "I'm looking at Airbnb. It's too late to bother your sister. There's a little apartment about a half a mile away. A hundred bucks a night. Let's go."

I didn't argue with her. We needed sleep, period, after such a long week, and with Faye needing to get up early in the morning. In five minutes, we were in the Jeep Cherokee and flitting off with a pair of duffels in the backseat. I had to crane my eyes to stay awake, but we got into the Bnb, no problem; it was just a little ground-level flat, two-bedroom, open concept, beautiful hardwood floors, a smart TV, incense sticks on a white mantlepiece, laminated welcome note, silver fridge, a spa-themed bathroom with an overhead shower faucet. "I may have to call the uncle," I said, rubbing my eyes and turning on the TV.

"The uncle?"

"Timmy's uncle. The pest guy."

"Timmy's got an uncle who exterminates pests?"

"That's what he said. I'll call him tomorrow. We won't have to deal with it anymore."

"Watching TV?"

I looked at the floating Roku screen and turned the TV off.

"No."

"Good. Cuz I need to go to bed. Now."

Staying in an Airbnb makes me feel like I'm slightly invading someone else's house, while wooing me over just enough to get me comfortable. The point is, though, that this is *not* our house, because our house comes with mice in the walls, and we have to sleep, damn it. We didn't dawdle. We threw off our clothes, clapped off the lights, and collapsed into the downy king to discover that it was a waterbed. Faye sighed with pleasure; my brain, mushed from exhaustion, settled into a soup of relief, and I thought our troubles might be over. For now.

I was almost asleep. I mean, *almost* asleep. So close to the precipice that when the sound, soft at first, met my covered ears, it snapped me awake and had me upright once again in the pitch blackness. A few cars sidled by outside, and the shadow of a guffawing clan of late-night outcasts shimmered in the living room window. But no, that wasn't it. I held my breath. Faye was already asleep. There it was again, that *scratching,* the skittering of paws on drywall. This time it sounded like there were even more than at our house.

"You're kidding," I whispered into the void. "You've *got* to be kidding me."

I wanted to wake up Faye so she could share in the disbelief, but she was solidly conked out and needed the rest. I hopped out of the bed and peered down the hallway to find nothing out of the ordinary. I mopped my chin with my hand and scratched what was left of my hair at the back of my head.

It's the invisible things in our lives that terrify us the most. Why is that? A noise without a known source has to be on the list of top ten things we humans are the most scared of. When I was a boy back in our summer home upstate, my brother and I shared a room and yours truly has a history of insomnia. Late one night in July, the cicadas going crazy outside in the trees on our little plot of land, I thought I heard someone walking around in the attic not four feet above my head. There was a trapdoor leading to the attic, which turned into a staircase when you pulled the string, and I remember the next morning, trembling and with a hatchet, venturing up into the heat to have a look around. Nothing. I told my dad, who begrudgingly went up a little later on and poked around the cardboard boxes, mopping his forehead. "There's nothing here, son," he said. "Nothing to be afraid of."

My father said that a lot. Nothing to be afraid of. Nothing to be afraid of. That consoled me as a kid, and I believed him like any kid believes his father. I really believed him, as if existentially, no single entity in the universe, seen or unseen, could cause me any harm. Now, though, while stoic and a Bonafide professional, I've learned to be afraid of just about everything. Getting fired. Getting divorced. Losing my house *to* a fire. Getting hit by a rogue Prius taxi. (It happened to a guy just last month, by the way. He survived. Just some bruised ribs.) Messing up a monthly report. Spilling coffee on my new shirt. We still hear things in the attic and wish our fathers would come to check things out for us. Maybe if I was a father, myself, I wouldn't be so afraid. But that's stupid.

I went into the living room after closing the bedroom door and watched some TV at a low volume. It wasn't loud enough to disturb Faye nor to hide the sounds of the scuttles. So, I just stayed up, not wanting to wake up my sleeping wife, not wanting to try to sleep for fear that something might come out of the walls and tickle our legs. Who knows? I'm a sensible, modern man.

The rest of the night passed in something of a haze. Maybe you know the feeling. When you're so tired but you know tonight's not the night you're going to get any sleep. There's a Coldplay song about that, I think. I got up at one point to explore the kitchen, upturning nil but some decaf coffee pods, which I brewed in the Keurig and sipped, wincingly, by the window. Every so often I snuck back into the bedroom just to make sure Faye was okay, that no mice nibbled her toes or nested in her hair. She was still deep asleep, hadn't moved a muscle. And all night, it was just scuttle, scuttle, scuttle. Do mice never sleep? Maybe they're metaphors for this city, this culture, this ongoing grinding world, my own grinding mind.

Very rarely do I stay up all night. Back in college, sleeping less for five hours put me in something of a coma the next day. Others could swim their way through delirium on mere espresso shots. Not me. Faye's one of those caffeine dependents, actually; she'll sleep for thirty minutes, take a shot, and run herself into the ground fifteen hours later after a full day of analytics and meetings and scratching her ankle with her high heels. We need to rest. No? And rest for the *both* of us, not singularly, having our circadian rhythms split. One exhausted man, one well-kept woman. . .it doesn't comply with the demands of a young marriage.

I fell asleep for about thirty minutes right before dawn broke, and woke up, bleary-eyed, brain a botch of unthinking stew, with a dull gray light on my couch-laden body. The Airbnb was quiet. Had I dreamed about the mice? Maybe. I didn't have the luxury of having Faye as an ear witness. A taxi honked its way through the silence and softened after a whooshing Doppler effect. Saturday. This was the day a working man sleeps in until nine after a ten-hour stint of genuine sleep, but I had never felt worse after a long night in my life. It was so bad that my limbs didn't obey my brain. I couldn't get up. For a second, it seemed I might be paralyzed. But there was still that wakefulness, way down deep, the heart behind the plywood, skittering with mouse feet, that eventually leveraged me into a sitting position and had me facing the morning light.

"Faye?" I called weakly. "Faye? Let's go away for the weekend."

III.

My parents have owned a cabin upstate for about thirty years, which is just a couple trips round the sun longer than I've been alive. These days they tend to prefer the vacation homes and Miami and Maine, and so most of the time the cabin remains empty on the edge of the Hudson River.

We took the train out there after Faye got coffee with her friend and checked on the house briskly to find it still in perfect order and hopped in the car to take the two-hour drive northward into wilderness and forestry. Faye was kind enough to drive. I slept on the way out there and woke up only as the car tires crunched over the familiar pattern of gravel driveway leading to the cabin. The structure sits well within the forest and is fairly separate from other cabins and establishments. There are the rocking chairs on the front porch, the small stone firepit in the yard, long unused and nearly full of fallen maple leaves, the blue shed on the other side of the driveway, collecting rust at the bases, and the silent doorway with that brass knocker in its dead center. Now *this* is a place where mice might very well roam free and probably *should*. So, if I was to hear them that night, I wouldn't be surprised. There. That was the plan. Now we would have some peace and quiet either way.

"Spontaneous trip," said Faye. "I'm glad we did it. Sorry you couldn't sleep last night."

"Maybe I'll sleep here."

She opened the cabinets and fridge, assessing inventory. There wasn't much, like we expected, but we'd picked up some groceries on the way.

"I just feel like, mice or no mice, we maybe needed to get out-for a little bit. Work being like it has, you know."

"Work is murder!" cried Faye. We don't usually talk about work in our domestic lives, but we can both feel it simmering, like slow-cooking ramen noodles, beneath the surface of our discourse. The fridge and pantry stocked, the bed linens dusted, the back patio swept and restored to order, the view of the lake finely tuned between a pair of pine trees, the trail still well trafficked by deer hooves, it all resembled harmony, a real day off. Quiet.

We walked down to the lake and splashed in the shallows. I climbed halfway up a tree. Faye laughed at me from below. We were like kids, giggling and snorting and ribbing. We skipped rocks and walked up a way to a dock where we lay on our bellies to stare at the rippling water. I like the faint fish smell and crisp aqua, the earthiness of it, and the little bit of breeze making the lake shiver. It's definitely been too long since we've been here. Call me sentimental. It's been way too long. Tired as I still was, I could feel the deeper tiredness, the city type of tiredness, the sixty-hour week kind of tiredness, ebb from my fingers and toes like it was bitter molasses. We were having a good time. And for the time being, we both forgot about the mice and the busted window back home.

We lit a fire in the cabin and curled up next to it with cups of tea and talked.

"This is nice," she said.

"Yeah. Been too long since we've just, you know, just gotten away."

"Maybe the mice were trying to tell us something."

"And the broken window?"

"Weird. Very weird. But we don't have to think about it right now."

I stoked the logs with the kindler and rested my chin on my knees. Faye lay on her stomach with her chin resting on her interlocked fingers and her caramel brown eyes dancing with the inky reflections of the fire. We were quiet for a long time. We chose not to check our phones the whole time we lay like that. That's not like us.

Later that night, we were side by side on the queen-sized bed when the wind picked up and something, whether a critter or another little tempest, scraped against the wall. This time it sounded like it came from the attic out of all places. Faye was already asleep. Not me. Once again, I was on the verge of slumber.

I plodded into the living room, found the old trapdoor, and climbed upstairs. There was nothing up there except some folded tarps in the corner, crusted with pine needles, an edger, my dad's pair of old Danner boots, and a wooden rocking chair. It smelled like dry pine and leather. I stood there for a second, eyes adjusting to the darkness, but it wasn't long before I found the source of the scratching. A branch from the old tree that hangs over the back patio brushed against the little attic window all up and down the south side of the house. I tilted my head and gave a little laugh. No, the mystery of the critters in the walls was not solved, nor was the weirdness of the broken window dissected. Who knows. Maybe some troubled young man hopped the fence and punched the glass or some leprechaun from the haunted past is getting revenge on modernity by knuckling everyone's drywall. But I crouched there in the darkness nonetheless and stared at the tree branch in the moonlight and remembered my father, remembered some voice that was older than me. What had he told me, again? I listened to the wind and breathed. Just breathed.

I stepped on a mouse trap on my way out of the attic. I'll let you guess what kind.

The Heel

Dan was twelve years old when he went out to hunt with Dad in the bumbler, that old metal hunk of a Ford from '85, Dan in the front seat and his crazy brother Chip crouched in the truck bed, a stowaway. Imagine dawn and its notes of blue making a mesh in the oak trees. Imagine a creek running like a church aisle through the woods as the truck stuttered on the gravel road and Dad said to Dan, "We're here. Grab your gun from the back seat."

Chip, on the other hand, was only eight years old, and he'd have his chance to shoot doves and quail in the winter of his defining year. You better believe each of these boys was due a real honest chance to prove mettle. But Chip had snatched low-hanging fruit and it would cost him, because he couldn't hide, not when Dad walked back to the truck bed to fetch his best boots, for there was the younger brother, shivering without a parka, wearing a measly pair of athletic slides, nose a red nub.

"The hell you doing?"

"I, uh, wanted to come along! Mom said I could!"

"That's a bunch of bull. The *hell* you wanted to come!" Dad got Chip by the scruff and settled him in the backseat with all the blankets and old bags of beef jerky. He muttered, "*Mom told me I could.* Good Lord if that ain't a bumming lie if I ever heard one.

You're outta control. Tryna blame your own mother even when she ain't here. Lord Almighty."

Dan, in the meantime, was stamping his boots on the gravel, furious. He bunched his chapped lips together till their scabs broke and bled and gripped the cold metal of his gun as if to brandish the butt against his young brother's noggin. This was Dan's morning. *His* moment. This kind of thing doesn't happen more than once, you have to understand. A boy becomes a man only once in this family. You can't mess this up. So, Chip cozied into the blankets all miserable with a bunch of beef jerky, and Dad put his parka over the kid, cussing all the while, and Dan glowered like a dying star in his new leather boots and the shotgun. He didn't know what Chip's punishment might be. To jump the gun on such a sacred occasion, though. Well, it was almost too much to swallow.

"He wasn't supposed to come," said Dan.

"He ain't coming," said Dad, whose lungs were like twin steam engines, puffing out blue. "He ain't coming and it's all right. We drove thirty minutes to get here and we're here. So it's all right."

Dad checked Dan's gun to make sure it had shells, was on the safety, and that he was holding it right, cradling it with the barrel downward and away from any human flesh, and whispered, "All right. We'll have to cross the creek. Woods get thick. They'll be all in the cedars and oaks, okay? 'Member. With the doves you can wait till they flutter up. Quail might just run for it. You let 'em have it and we'll have a big lunch made out of 'em later today. Okay?"

"Okay."

They crossed the creek using a pair of stones Dad had put there a long time ago when he first started coming out to this edge of the ranch, and the stones were still there, still solid, cupped with strings of eely moss on the sides, making them look like the heads of some river gods turned to rock. Dan slipped just a tad on the second stone and felt the cold wet seep through the tongue of his boot, just where the leather was barely parted, exposing some sock. Dad turned around and put a finger to his lip. Dan turned around to make sure Chip wasn't crawling around after them. But no. The forest green truck was dead quiet on the side of the gravel road, with the gray trees making a film behind it, gemmed with layers of sunshine.

Pretty soon, after the creek and after Chip was out of sight, after Dan had simmered down a little bit, they knelt there in the cold wet leaves, crispy round the edges from the frost, and watched that patch of world wake up. If it ever slept, that is; Dan got the sense that these trees had night watches, that their knobs and roots never stopped scoping and probing earth, air, and sky, that the trickle of water behind them, while it traditionally ebbed and flowed with the ways of water, was a sort of creature, always wriggling, stomaching memories of the briar patches, the rolls of morning fog, the boy and the man who crossed, who crouched, who waited.

"Be real still," whispered Dad. "Watch for movement. That's the key. Your eyes respond best to movement."

He was wide eyed, alert, ready for the appearance of various beasts: the gray squirrel, the nosing opossum, the unctuous raccoon. He had imagined himself in this moment and in this specific place for a long time, almost ever since he was self-conscious. For years he was just a boy on the edge of his first hunt, yearning to bag some birds, bring home the booty, feed the whole family. His father's own young eyes, blue and blinking, were settled on the woods, the red beard like a living bush, like a part of the forest furniture. Dan imitated his father's epic gaze. They sat up against a dead oak tree, which had a bunch of knobs and holes big enough to put an arm in. In front of them lay the tangles of trees and briars and some kind of nettle that had stayed green amidst the frost.

Of course, if you've ever been hunting, you get that the excitement doesn't always plop down in front of you like Christmas dinner. Five minutes passed and pretty much nothing of import occurred. Dad didn't move nary a muscle. Dan got to the point where he felt like he had to move, to kick, punch air, maybe even yell, around minute eleven, and had to bite his painfully chapped lips some more to ebb off the urge. Dad, though? A picture of stoicism. He was quiet and smile-free when he woke up and when he came back at the end of the day in his dirty work boots. A silent man who never talked about his own childhood, tragic that it was, as Mom told him. "He's been through a lot, honey," she said. "There's a reason you never met your grand daddy."

"Why? What happened to him?"

"We don't talk about it with you and Chip. Not yet. Okay?"

And when Dad came in after work, Mom would be stirring something instant in the kitchen, table marginally set with porcelain plates and white napkins, a fly or two a-buzz under the table light. Chip would already be at the table, drawing on print paper with a pair of crayons, and Dad would walk over to Mom and put his hands briefly on her shoulders and then reach for a glass in the cupboard. He always liked to fill up his own glass of water.

They sat in the leaves for about thirty more minutes. Every so often, Dad would sniff and rub his nose on the sleeve of his Carhartt. And Danny would flex his toes in his boots just to move some part of his body without breaking the perfect peace of the forest. His butt, despite the long underwear, was starting to get wet. He wondered if the dumb birds would ever descend or if maybe they were all skirting the humans from a distance, watching them rot. He almost posed this question to Dad when, alas, brown little dove alighted on the spindly branch of a mulberry tree about twenty feet away and cocked its head at the sunrise. Dad clutched Dan's arm and nodded. "Slow," he whispered. "Raise it slow." And Dan did raise it slowly as if he was raising a fly swatter to squash an insectoid offender on some tabletop. He cocked the 16 gauge and stared down its barrel, trying not to tremble, flicking off the safety and taking deep breaths. There she was, the poor thing, right in his sites.

"All right," whispered Dad. "Shoot. Now."

Dan heard the words clearly. But he didn't shoot the bird as she blinked and tufted her feathers in the sunshine. Many years later, he couldn't exactly tell anyone *why* he didn't shoot, since he shot plenty of other birds later on in his life without much of a second thought. But right then and there, he just watched the bird through the sights and couldn't bring himself to pull the little trigger. Even when he was on the verge of doing it, of shooting, of biting his boyish tongue, Chip sneezed a few feet behind them and the dove fluttered up into the trees and was gone.

"*Chip,*" Dad hissed. "Jesus, you scared the heck outta me."

They both scrambled to their feet to address the scallywag, and Dan's finger was still settled on the trigger, and the safety was still turned off, and his father's booted heel was right in the gun's sights when Dan tripped on a root and fired the missile hell-ward.

The shell blew a chunk off Dad's heel, and the force of the shot flipped him on his stomach, huffing and hacking and grasping the roots of the old oak tree, and Chip began to scream as if *he* had been shot, which is exactly what Dan thought had happened the five seconds after he fired the gun. He threw the gun into the leaves. Then, he fell down again, backwards. The sky wheeled above his head in its selfsame blue gaze, until he managed to crawl like a soldier in no man's land to his father's quivering side. Half of his father's right boot was blown off. The stumpy flesh bled into the leaves, and the man, now over his initial shock, breathed shallow breaths into the morning.

"You *shot* him!" yelped Chip.

"Are *you* shot?" Dan said.

"No I ain't shot! Daddy's shot! I said *Daddy's* shot!"

"Boys!" Dad hissed. "You get me up on my feet, all right? You help me back to the truck. Dan!" He winced and sweat popped on his brow. "You gotta drive. I can't drive. Ahhh, okay? Okay?"

"Dad, Dad, I'm sorry, so sorry, so sorry, I don't why I didn't shoot the bird, don't know why I didn't shoot the dumb bird, don't know why—"

"Get me up! Get me up!"

Chip and Dan burrowed under their father's arms and struggled to get him up on one foot, and then started the long hobble back to the truck.

"What did you do?" cried Chip. "Why didn't ya shoot the bird?"

Dad gritted his teeth so hard that the tendons in his jaws gave shape to the outline of his beard. Dan was just trying to breathe, let alone say anything, and Chip kept up his sobbing.

The truck, when they reached it, gleamed in the morning sunshine. A group of quail ran across the road just to rub it in, purple flanks catching light like fire. Chip got the passenger door open and they got Dad in, who held up his foot as it poured blood on the mat. Dad rifled through the glove compartment and came up with a couple of oily rags that he used as a makeshift tourniquet for the heel. Dan hopped into the driver's seat with the keys and started up the truck. Chip sobbed in the backseat.

"You shot him! You shot him!"

"Chip, shut up! Shut *up*!"

Dan didn't know where he was going, so he drove home, all the way home, the opposite direction of the hospital, and Dad didn't even try to direct the boy, didn't even lift a hand of correction. He was too busy clenching his teeth, feeling the whites of his eyes roll upward in searing pain as the passenger side mat became a little colony of blood puddles. It was Mom who took Dad to the hospital right after Dan and Chip collapsed on the ground right after the cattle guard. She didn't even ask what happened. She just ran outside and hopped into the truck, spun it round like she was in a Nascar race, and zoomed off with the man without so much as a, "Wait here!"

And they had to wait about eight hours when it was all said and done. Chip and Dan. Only Dan decided he wouldn't twiddle his thumbs on the front porch. No, he chased Chip to the backyard first. Then he chased him all the way to the back pasture, scattering some cows, where he rolled his ankle and got a face-full of burrs and briars. After that, in his defeat, he limped after his brother until they both ended up in the front yard by the cattleguard, leaning on their knees and crying for breath.

"You weren't supposed to come!"

"It isn't fair you got to go!"

"It's *your* fault!"

"No, it's *your* fault! You *always* leave me out!"

Dan limped inside and slammed the door to his bedroom and cried it out on his bed until 2 p.m. rolled around and his parents came back home from the hospital.

When the headlights appeared at the end of the driveway, both boys forgot their feud and headed fitfully outside. They crouched behind the barn together, feeling equally indicted, fearing the worst forms of punishment.

"We're dead," said Chip. "We're dead men!"

"Shut up!" Dan massaged his ankle and leaned his head against the tin wall. The sunset made a pale pink rash above the prairie, and a flock of swallows made a fell swoop against its color and plummeted low to nestle in a range of huddled birch trees. They listened. The truck had stopped and their parents' low voices could be heard as the two of them shuffled through the front door. Dan clenched his fists. Chip quietly cried. This meant certain grounding. It meant no more basketball team for Dan. It meant no more dove hunting, that was for sure, at least not for another century or so. Chip's rite of passage would almost certainly be cancelled.

The backdoor opened a couple minutes later, and their father shouted cleanly into the open air, "Boys?"

Neither one of them responded. They just hugged their knees and begged God for peaceful deaths. "Boys? Where are you?" The clack of a pair of crutches grated the silent winter night. At least he hadn't bled out and died. This was bad enough, but Dan didn't think he could manage living with accidental patricide. It was Chip's fault!

Now the crutches crossed the backyard, with Dad giving rhythmic grunts every time he hoisted himself off the ground.

"Where are you going, honey?" said Mom.

"Going to find 'em."

"Where do you think they went?"

"I don't know. Maybe they ran away."

His voice, although pained and weary, sounded more in keeping with the tone of a man who has lost a treasure that was supposed to steward. This lightened the boys up a little, but they still didn't stand up or say anything. It was dark enough now for the lads to go undetected behind the barn, melded like a couple of lawnmowers that haven't been used in years, so when Dad finally rounded the corner, he had to struggle for the flashlight in his back pocket. When he turned it on and pointed, there were his sons, crouched and crying, never to be the same.

"Oh," said Dad. "There you are." Just like that, the wounded man let his crutches fall, and sat down against the tin barn, too, and turned off the flashlight. Coyotes yipped somewhere out in the darkness.

"Turns out it wasn't that bad," he said. "Most of my foot is still intact."

"I'm sorry, Dad," said Dan. "I didn't mean to. I should have just shot the bird. I don't know why I didn't just *shoot* the bird."

"I'm sorry, too!" yelped Chip.

Dad cleared his throat and leaned his head against the wall. "You know," he said. "I haven't said to this to either of you yet, and I wasn't planning on it until you were older, but when I was around your age, Dan, I was driving a tractor and let my little brother ride with me, even though I said it was dangerous, and we hit a bump, and. . ." He swallowed and was quiet for a few seconds. "We took him to the hospital but by then it was too late. I can't tell you how hard my daddy hit me that night, or how loud he howled at me. I can't tell you how awful that experience was." The boys were petrified now.

"But I made a promise," he went on. "I made a promise that if I were to ever have sons, that even thought I might not say a lot, or like I might come across like I don't care, that if they were to do something terrible on accident, that I wouldn't hate them for it. So Dan, hear me when I say it—you should've been more careful, but it was an accident. Do you hear me?"

"Yes, sir."

"And Chip. You shouldn't have been there, but it ain't your fault, either. Do you hear me?"

"Yes, sir."

"All right." Dad struggled to his feet, wincing, and Dan got up and scrambled for his crutches.

"Thank you, son."

They all stood up now, making each other's faces out in the dimness, and the father, despite the crutches, spared his arms to take his two sons in. Both Dad and Dan had their wounded feet lifted off of the ground.

Invisible Sun

Sam got off the train and stood on the cold pavement of the station platform and checked his pockets for his keys. He brought them out in a jangle and walked down the sidewalk toward his apartment building on Harbor Street, as if this was somehow just a repetition of his daily routine. In truth, he had endured another eternal day at the office trying to nab the dealers of a new drug going rampant on Luxley's streets and the streets of surrounding towns, but after raiding a couple of homes, scouring the abandoned underground train depots, and even establishing a curfew, the stuff kept getting out and gripping the whole lifeless urban area. And it was a problem for everyone. The sun, hidden above the manmade clouds of the city, grayly shone. Yes, a real problem.

It was cold even for Luxley for the month of March, with another slate gray sky brewing snowfall, almost ready to spew. Sam drew his collar above his ears and matted his cap over his hair. The apartment buildings on Harbor were squat, concrete, homogeneous, dark-windowed, with the avenue lamps already lit up. A coffee house, one of the few rejections of the city's brutalist essence, hummed with acoustic guitars and overflowed with the tempting smell of espresso, chocolate, warm company. The coffee shop, the one bohemian locus point on the block, didn't make sense inside this gritty coliseum of gray stone.

Sam needed to sleep, though. No caffeine at this hour. No nostalgic yuppies in beanies and scarves tonight. He needed to clear his head with whiskey and a cigarette and maybe a cold shower just to check reality.

He couldn't get the last interview of the day out of his head as he bustled into his apartment and shucked off his work clothes. Just imagine a purple sweater and jeans sitting down with a cup of bad coffee, a blue beanie, one that reminded him acutely of the one his ex-wife Candie used to wear, rotating on top like a crown as the invisible woman slurps and clears her throat. That's what his last interview of the day looked like.

"Name?" Sam had asked.

"Um. . .Jessica."

Had she forgotten her own name? And what about that voice? She sounded like a bad voice actor auditioning for a play.

"What can you tell me about this drug?"

"Nothing you don't already know, Detective."

"All I know is that it turned you invisible. Are you happy about that? Is that *why* you took this substance?"

"Happy? Happy is so out of vogue, Detective. Happy is such a relic. We oughta give it up, you know. Being happy. Never works, does it?"

In theory, he could have met this "Jessica" at the local grocery store. He might have passed her at some point at the local park, or maybe she had even shown up on one of the dating apps he was trying out—to his embarrassment. Her voice sounded half-way familiar to him, like she really was trying to sound like some-one else. Most voices in Luxley sounded more or less the same: Roughly male and robotic or roughly female and robotic, sharing the same lilts, speaking statements that sounded like questions. So, it was noteworthy to hear a unique voice, one that seemed to have evaded the pressures of mass media. He remembered the floating piece of candy in her invisible hands. She teased the wrapping but never put the candy in her mouth.

His best guess, after they took the woman back to the wait-ing room with the other invisible addicts, was that some rogue scientist had concocted the drug, done a deal with a couple of inner-city outfits, and boom! Who could stop the crime wave now? They knew, so far, that the drug, which came in a simple form of a blue pill as small as an ibuprofen tablet, offered ecstasies that exceeded heroin. Whoever made this thing knew the secrets of both chemistry and alchemy. This stuff vaulted people to the high heaven and back. Of course, though, you had the side effects. Take more than ten of those pills and you started to fray around the edges. Become a bit transparent, like a dirty tarp. Take ten more, and you could probably get mistaken for a shadow cast by a streetlamp. Any more than that, and you were as good as gone, with just the clothes on your back to verify any palpability.

Sam poured himself a glass of water in his kitchen apartment, shaking his head at the inanity of all this, how stupefying and end-of-the-world all of this felt, and looked out the window. Pale light blanketed the hard stone floor. A man shouted nonsense a block down. Sam picked up a piece of mail on the counter and frowned. He hadn't picked up the mail on his way in, but the envelope, holding a bank statement, was dated from earlier that day. Maybe he *had* picked it up and just didn't remember. The day's weirdness was confusing his motor functions. He perused the bank statement and then plotted a simple dinner of leftover buttered chicken and asparagus and poured a hint of whiskey into his favorite tumbler before sitting in his chair by the front door, which sat across from his wife's old hanging hammock swing. He shook his head and propped his feet up on the footstool and contemplated turning on the TV. The place felt too quiet in stark contrast to all the talking he'd done that day. It felt like a cosmic vacuum cleaner had sucked all the air out of the apartment.

Sometimes after a long day, he talked to his wife. Today such talk felt apropos.

"Honey," he said, "in all my years, never chanced on a case like this. Only witnesses we have are self-reporting. They don't want to be this way. Must be a hell of a drug." The swing tilted a little, courtesy of the upstairs tenant stomping across the second floor.

"I don't know. I don't know if I believe in ghosts. But this drug's turning everybody into ghosts. *That* I can't deny." He downed the rest of the whiskey and wiped his mouth with the back of his wrist.

"Candie," he whispered, leaning forward. "It's days like this where I'd really like to *not* be by myself. You know? Theoretically, there could be someone standing right over there and I wouldn't notice it. Break in and entering cases have already quadrupled since the vanishing pill hit the streets. . .I guess, theoretically, *you* could be sitting there. Ha. What a stupid, crazy thought." He leaned back. He leaned forward. The swing was still suspended in its typical two feet above the floor, still contoured in the shape of his wife. Sam rubbed his forehead, put the strands of thinning salt and pepper hair back into place, and returned to the kitchen for another draught.

When Candie called him just under a year ago and told him she was leaving him and everything else, that she just couldn't give him what he wanted, that the papers were coming, he stood on the train station platform like he had just a few minutes earlier. Streams of hurried people had walked past him. They minded their own business. He minded his. And Sam never could explain why, but all he said in return was, "Thanks a lot, my friend," and from there, he got on his hands and knees and crawled the two blocks down Harbor Avenue. He could walk, yes. But the bipedal norm felt like an insult to the tragedy. He had to crawl, and cry, all the way through the stone jungle; the rebellious bohemians, even though they sang about their love for humanity and their rage against the machine in the proximate café, only glanced at the human caterpillar through the window and kept up the joviality.

"Grieving people sometimes need to talk to their lost loved ones," Mrs. Randall told him the week after in her therapy office. "It's okay. Go ahead. Talk to her, Sam."

"But she's not there. She's with someone else. Caught up with some bad people from L.A. She had a history of drug use before we met. I could have seen this coming. And she was using again, you know. Toward the end." He paused and bowed his head. "I don't know where she is. Just have wild guesses."

"I know. I know she's not there."

"It's funny, I guess, when you think about it," said Sam. "Not funny. God, I didn't mean to say *funny.* Just that we were having some problems, Candie and me. She'd stormed out of the house that morning and told me she was never coming back. And she never did."

"What were you arguing about?" Mrs. Randall was a wiry lady of fifty-three, with a kind tilt in her head, bright blue eyes that were made for the trade of understanding the broken, and lips that pursed in compassion whenever her beleaguered patient talked. She held no notebook. She clicked no pen on her doilies. There was an old painting of a gray fox in a glade of aspen trees above her desk behind her head.

"Having children," Sam had replied. He shook his head. No whiskey at the therapist's office. "I wanted. She didn't."

Every couple has their recurring scuffles, and this argument hung over all of them; living in this apartment versus a house outside of town, how much money to donate and how much to save toward the future house, whether getting out of detective work might calm Candie's nerves. Her father used to be a cop. She told Sam about how her father would tramp home after midnight and she would get up to watch him hang up the belt in the hallway, slowly, as if pantomiming a sloth. She didn't want that kind of life for Sam. Never did. One that forces you to slow down ordinary time before you have to go back into the craze. She also didn't want to put children in this cold new world, either. Especially not one where a third of its constituents are tangible ghosts, prone to revel wickedly in their newfound liberties.

Sam went back to the kitchen window. His apartment complex was shaped like a square "U," and his two-bedroom setup came with a view of the outdoor common area which featured nothing but a tree, park bench, and a chunk of the street a block away. A swinging gate, a self-functioning bicycle, or a shattered window would tell him that these ghosts were alive and roaming the city with impunity.

He closed his eyes.

And what do you know. The door opened.

It opened and then *closed* so fast that he wondered if it even happened in the first place. He turned around and felt the breath of cold air mix with the interior room temperature and so knew, now, that someone had certainly slipped inside.

"Who's there?"

The invisible visitor said nothing. The chill whiff integrated with the room and Sam wondered whether he should charge at the door or skirt nimbly to the side until the intruder knocked over a vase or scuffled the rug. He compressed himself against the wall and reached into the nightstand by Candie's floating chair. He produced a tiny black revolver that looked like it was last brandished by Humphrey Bogart in a black and white movie. Why hadn't he locked the door? Was he expecting someone? He always locked the door. Especially these days.

The old cuckoo clock ticked on the wall in his bedroom but besides that all he could hear was the high din of his own ears.

"I know you're in here," he said, scanning the room with the gun. "I know you're probably trying to rob me. Maybe you're cleaning out the whole street before the weekend. Go ahead and make your move. I know it'll get messy."

The other cops at the office told him that the drug could make the patient cough randomly and violently, but he didn't hear as much as a sniffle in the living room. He went into the kitchen with the gun held against his chest and looked at his smartphone on the kitchen table. Maybe he would call the police, but he *was* the police. And where was his evidence to prove a ghost was in the room with him? A thermal sensor might be the best bet at this point.

Maybe I imagined it, he told himself. It was possible. These long days, disorienting conversations with the half-dead, and recurring dreams about Candie along with his general cluelessness over her location had his body all unnaturally attuned. Maybe warm felt cold and savory almost sweet, like by virtue of all these druggies gone invisible everything else in life should flip to its opposite. He picked up the bank statement again and then finally returned to his recliner across from Candie's old chair.

It hung just inches from the ground and the peg from which it hung creaked with weight. He stiffed and pointed the gun at the hammock chair.

"Who's *there*?"

No answer. Whoever it was must have felt like a popsicle since total invisibility meant being totally naked.

"Candie?" He said her name as if asking a celebrity for an autograph. The hammock swing gave another tilt. The tenant upstairs had gone dormant. "Stay quiet if it's you. I promise I won't lunge." It was only after the mysterious stranger obeyed the invective that the mix of emotions broiled in his gut. The latent sediments of rejection began to swirl. Beads of sweat populated his scalp and the back of his neck burned as hot as a dungeon torch.

"Candie," he whispered. "You have to talk to me."

He'd been talking all day with these invisible patients, rendering into basically nothing by those pills, and thought that he'd concluded his last interview at the office. The best they could tell him was that they had all picked up the drug from different people and that no one seemed to know where it came from. One more interview, he guessed.

He leaned back and put his skinny hands on his knees. "Okay. Then I'll talk to you. The counselor told me to do it, so I guess I will. You know I'd take you back. I've wanted you to come back every single day since you've left! And if that's actually you right in front of me, then you might be laughing inside. Me, expressing some kind of vulnerability. I know that doesn't make sense. That you never felt like I opened up. My job taught me to keep it all under a lid. Solve the case. Detect the spider in the corner. Squash it and move onto the next. What am I supposed to do? Fall on the floor now and shout how much I miss you? I've done that plenty of times on my own."

An ambulance whined a mile down and turned down Harbor Street until it threw its fractal rays of blue and red across Sam's face and made the hammock chair look like a Christmas disco ball.

"Candie?"

The ambulance turned around another corner and almost crashed with a street crosser on its way. Sam tried to keep talking but couldn't string anymore words together. He was afraid. It fell on him like a dump of icy water, the fear. He couldn't stay there a second longer, and just about sprinted outside and followed the waning sound of the ambulance into the cold dusk.

He left the door unlocked. A burglar would steal everything, but an invisible wife might at least leave a note. At least this way he might know one way or the other.

He went around the street corner where the ambulance had rattled and vanished. Maybe he'd find a clue to the mystery along the way. Maybe they'd found someone bleeding, only the blood would look like it simply encapsulated air as molasses coats a fragile cake. It might be that he would crack the case as a civilian and not with his magnifying glass in hand.

The ambulance's red and blue cacophony of color and noise lofted way off on the other side of Luxley. He stopped after going about a half a mile down the street and looked straight up into the foggy sky past the low skyscrapers and the naked elm trees. When he leveled his head and pulled a loose glove back into place, a child ran across the avenue against his mother's wishes a scant ten yards in front of him. The boy wore a puffy blue jacket and gray sweatpants, and the woman was brown-haired, plain, perhaps all alone in the world. Her face was ashen and flashed like a sad moon under the streetlamp.

"Tony!" she shouted. She didn't catch up with the runaway until the he made it clear across the street and had stooped to investigate a nigh-invisible object on the sidewalk. The boy had found a quarter on the ground and held it up to verify the treasure to his mother. The woman held him to her chest and patted the boy's back. Meanwhile, the little boy held the quarter up to the streetlight and ogled at its majesty. Sam started to back away, almost tripped over a sewage grate, and had to spin to save himself from a fall.

He walked back down the street and opened his own door in a rush, not wanting to drag out the unveiling of what he would find inside, and he half-expected the whole place to be ransacked. It wasn't. The apartment was still in order. His empty tumbler still set on the stand beside his recliner. Candie's floating hammock, no longer weighted, barely shifted from overhead tramping. Sam went into the bedroom and swept out his phone to call the sheriff back at the office.

"James?"

"I thought you'd had it for the day, Sammy."

"I want to shift focus. Or add a focus. If you don't work with me I'll quit the force."

"Well, what the hell is it?"

"A cure!" Sam ran a hand through his hair. "We have to find a cure." He didn't know what a sheriff could do about a "cure."

"A cure? For the vanishing drug?"

"That's what I want."

James wiped his mustache on the other end.

"Uhhh. . .well, I'm not really a drug whiz, cap. You know someone affected?"

"Maybe."

"Well, here's the deal. Now this isn't official, so don't quote me on this, but we got a call today. It was a mother saying her son got on the pill a few months ago but came back just last Friday."

"Yeah?"

"It freaked her out at first, of course, seeing just a pair of pants and a jacket sitting there, but he said he was scared, you know, and didn't know what to do. She didn't know what to do either, of course, so she just found his hand and held it for a while. What do you know, his sister and father came in after a while and put their hands on him, too, one on the shoulder, one on the top of his head, and his mother told me that after a while of just touching her son, they could sort of start to see him again."

"Really?"

"Again, don't quote me on it. But we're at the point where these addicts are going to want to find a way back. The lady said that in an hour she could see her son's eyes again. What do you know about that?"

Sam lowered the phone without hanging up, the silence of his apartment pulsing like an ever-present heart, and blinked, startled, at the sight of the blue-covered bed below him. A piece of candy, still in its plastic blue wrapping, lay on his wife's old side of the mattress. Or was it a cough drop? No, it was candy, like you would give kids at Halloween, dressed up as a ghost. In any case, Sam had never put it there.

A Dog Named Job

THE city of Nodding had built the eight bullet trains in case the day of the bomb ever came, and when the day did come, to the horror of all, Jennings was at Pet Smart to buy dog food.

Catastrophes happen in history books. That's what everybody in town unconsciously assumed. They happen to other people in other countries, not ours. They happen to strangers in faraway lands. Jennings spent a few years on the Oklahoma-Kansas border as a child. Tornadoes scarred the springtime earth every April but tended to demolish *other* towns in the region—never his. This amounted to the law of basic narcissism, and he knew that. He did. It wasn't rational to assume the worst could never happen to *him*, but the unspoken law had more or less stood the test of time over his thirty-three years. Now the eight trains, each pointing due north, took off their wrapping paper and began to flood with passengers.

He stood outside Pet Smart with the dog food over his shoulder, like he was a nomad at the tail-end of a caravan in the desert, when the first siren started, the line of cars began to bunch and extend like a contorted spring along the fast-food chains, outlet stores, and broken-down warehouses with the plywood covering the windows serving as early premonitions of the inevitable. The missiles were on their way, and some people—the temperamentally fearful and conspiratorial—had already gotten the heck out of dodge.

Jennings leaped into his car, avoiding the cars that caterwauled through the lot, and decided without second thought that he would race to get Job, his ancient greyhound, before heading to the train station. He also wanted to grab some other treasures from the sinking ship if he could. He was like Lot's wife, looking back on the doomed city and about to become a pillar of salt. He took deep breaths as he waited for the light to turn green and the horns honked, people shrieked, and the sky adopted an imaginary green shade that reflected everyone's inner guts. It was finally happening. No more drills, no more conjectures, no more jaded warnings of the end of the world. This was the real deal.

The eight trains were long and spacious enough, supposedly, to fit all thirty thousand people in town. They could also bolt off to 300 miles per hour in just seconds, heading straight for Canada, with titanium-layered exteriors that were supposed to reject vestiges of radiation. Jennings wondered though, as he pulled into the driveway of his rental house, if there would be enough time for everyone to even *board*. There was no time to wonder for long. He raced inside the front door with the dog food over his shoulder and yapped, "Job! Job! Here Job!"

He set the food down by the door and the dog's empty metal bowl and checked his phone. He had no relatives in town, thankfully. Most of them still lived down in Little Rock except for his younger sister, who was just finishing up her undergraduate studies at the University of Florida. He hoped the swamp was immune from danger.

"Where are ya, buddy? We gotta go!"

He fluttered into the kitchen. Egg remains still crusted the edges of an iron skillet. The pleasant gray light from the morning had matured into a full-on apricot sun dance. It was an otherwise perfect afternoon. The checked tile hearkened back to Cold War days when every kid in America was taught that ducking beneath a desk would shelter them from the atomic blast. The fridge was speckled with photos of family reunions, Christmas cards, his brother Jody's wedding, and Job.

"C'mere boy!" Typically, the dog would be laying in front of the backdoor on his faded blue pad. Now the pad was empty, matted down by years of dog dreams with a sediment of gray fur making pale waves on its edges.

"Job!"

He ran upstairs and knocked a painting off the wall. The sirens must have scared the dog blind. The ancient pup only ran to safety during thunderstorms. The last time the sky had spat hail, Job managed to limp up the stairs and cuddle at the foot of the bed while Jennings slept through the whole affair. So far, though, the room yielded no sign of canine. His bed was an unmade tangle of blue covers and sheets. A phone call rattled in his pocket from his mother. He answered it briskly as he looked under the bed and tossed the closet door open with his foot.

"Honey, oh honey, are you out of there? Please tell me you're safe!"

"Hey, Mom. I'm all right. It'll be all right. I'm on my way to the trains, like everybody else. You guys all right?"

"Well, we're out of the radius, but we're just worried sick for you. And if the grid gets hit—"

"I'm fine. It'll be fine."

"Oh honey, please let us know the second you're out of the blast range."

"Yeah. Yeah. I will. Tell Jody he still owes me a hundred bucks when you see him. I'm coming down to collect." The humor failed at the release. His mother said, "Ohh" and then he hung up after a quick, "Love you."

Job wasn't under the bed nor in the closet. He wasn't slumped over in the bathroom, and he wasn't crimped in the hot water compartment. He wasn't passed out in the tiny patch of backyard, and he wasn't anywhere in the living room. Jennings even checked under the *sink*.

"What in the world? Job! Job!"

Job had showed up on Jennings' doorstep three years earlier in a thunderstorm, looking so skinny, pitiful, and friendless that his new owner decided on something Biblical to do him proper homage. Jennings liked to say that he was dropped off by cruel men as a gift from God. Maybe both things can be true at the same time?

The sirens' whine, meantime, grew to an even higher pitch, as if the authorities were trying to rack up the dread. The President said just last week that if the enemy pressed the button, decided go full-on World War III, people in vulnerable locations would only have minutes to escape. Thank God, he said, the spending bill to develop high-speed trains of escape town with over 20,000 people.

"Job!"

He had to take the hunt outside. His apartment included a staircase, but overall was narrow as a beanstalk and hid just a few nooks and crannies big enough for a scared dog to fit in.

When he stumbled out the door, the last of the cars on the neighborhood block swerved around the corner, losing a coffee thermos out the passenger window as it zinged perilously close to the green street sign. It was a blue Honda Civic, slightly rusted at the hub caps, decorated with a Yellowstone National Park sticker on the dusty metal rump. He stopped on the driveway, Birkenstocks sideways on his feet, and gaped. It happened to be *his* car swerving, hitting the curb and going airborne until rattling back down and vanishing in the mid-afternoon ooze of sunshine. His car, his escape mode. He'd left the keys on the front seat, figuring he'd be in and out with the dog in a couple of minutes, and a passerby must've capitalized on the crisis and felt justified to save his own skin from destruction. For a moment, for several moments—a pure wasted minute, maybe—Jennings gaped at the empty street, saw his empty driveway in a quivering shade of red, and finally walked back inside.

His adrenaline seemed to reach a boiling point. All of his fight or flight impulses tipped over the edges of his mental membranes and then stultified. He couldn't seem to *move* anymore. In a punch, the old adage, that *other* people might get their car stolen on the edge of a nuclear apocalypse, evaporated. He went upstairs and looked out the window. He could actually see the eight golden trains two miles away, all lined up and gleaming, with the remaining dozens of passengers going all aboard for what might be the final ride of their lives. He ran back downstairs. "Job," he whispered. "Oh Job, where are you?"

Back outside, he jogged to the end of the block and peered down the road leading downtown. Empty as an old Christmas stocking. He banged on someone's front door. He even tried the lock on a nearby Sedan. Next, he flailed down the road and screamed for help, which was probably what he should have done right after the car was stolen. No one came out of their doors. No shop owner peered through the tinted glass. Where were all of the homesteaders hiding in their basements filled to the brim with gallons of water and gasoline? They were too far under to hear him. He called Sam from work. It instantly went to voicemail. He called five other friends in the area, all who failed to pick up. Everyone must have figured that their friends had all the necessary means of escape.

His final solution was to collapse in the middle of the street by Tommy's Bagel Stand and let his forehead touch the cool, shadowed cement. "Oh God," he whispered. "Dear God." The sirens had stopped now, replaced by a sinister form of silence that eventually evolved into a quiet rustling of the lines of ornamental pear trees planted up and down the sidewalks.

When he looked up, to his left, he was faced with the wooden doors of a chapel he passed every day on his way to work but had never actually entered. He wasn't particularly religious, although he'd been raised Methodist and always appreciated the high-domed curvatures of the church, the wooden arches and beams, the infinite wisdom of saints imbued in the sunlit puzzle pieces of the mosaic windows. He hurried inside the chapel, shocked it wasn't locked too, and took a seat at the back of the sanctuary, quietly sweating.

Maybe his childhood memories of church spurred him to go inside. Maybe a part of him imagined Job would be in here, wagging a tail at the altar, waiting for the end, even welcoming it with open paws. He didn't want to go back home, though, and felt as though somehow these ancient stone slabs might do better to protect him from the atomic blast than even the deepest cellar in the ground. This was the temple of wishful thinking, anyway, was it not? What better place was there to pretend that all was well and all manner of things shall be well?

He sat there, shivering, bowing his head, sometimes looking at the gleaming, colored windows and the wood cross about the choir chamber at the front of the room. He checked his phone to find that it had died, and that the screen had cracked from when he'd dropped it earlier on the streets trying to call people. No, he was alone now. Alone with light and silence. The missiles were coming, though. He could almost hear their distant whines as they seared through outer space before dipping downward toward Earth. They were supposed to hit just five miles east of the town. From that distance, the explosion would more than just level old Nodding. It would instantaneously turn it into a flat grid of dust. He would be an imprint on the earthy floor—maybe the only human dust shadow in the whole ghost town.

He figured now was the time to pray. He bowed his head, mouthed the words that he was sorry—for what, he wasn't sure—and then, to his shock, heard a door open and shut at the front of the sanctuary. His felt the impulse to hide behind the pew, which he did, only to peek over its edge a moment later to see an old man dressed in white pastoral robes holding a silver vase of water. He had long gray hair, a bulbous beard that sprayed out in its own atomic blast and was humming to himself. He went up to a pair of plants by the communion table and watered each of them with equity. He turned to a basin by the pulpit, which was ornately carved from some deep-hued pine and included a little mahogany staircase and poured the rest of the water into it. He picked up a duster from the front pew and dusted the communion table. And then, he held a hymnal up to his face and sang "All Creatures of Our God and King," all five verses, in a low soprano that rang off the ceilings and sunk into the stone walls. It seemed like a normal afternoon to him. It was just another light-filled day. The only other thing he did was get down on his knees on the blue carpet behind the communion table, pray out loud that God would have mercy, and then slip back inside to what was apparently his little office cove.

Should he knock? Should he replace the old man on the altar and pray, too?

Jennings got up to go to the altar, as if there were some holy incense for him to bathe in. Or maybe he would divert course, go into the office, and speak to the priest just to have the company of another person before the end of the world. But he stopped at the sound of scratching at the door behind him, followed by an oddly familiar whimper. He only ever heard that small sound during thunderstorms when he lay in bed with the bedroom door closed. Jennings turned around and opened the front door to find Job the dog with his head bowed, gray, matted hair looking almost identical to the locks of the old churchman. The sirens were still silent, a bird chirped in the boughs above his head, and the unmistakable whistling of a train sounded a mile away, getting closer.

Janice Cries Wolf

A werewolf tiptoed across the field when Janice went out to get the eggs from the coop. No one even noticed her when she came back inside, or maybe they were simply four whiskeys into their card game and couldn't even hear her say, "Dad, Dad, Dad!" So, she was ashen faced when she went to her room, petrified in her gut when she drew the curtains and put her little fists by the hot prongs of the heater on the wall. Dad's buddies were over at the house and Mom was working a late shift at Walgreen's. Janice saw it, though. No question. She saw it even now in her redheaded mind.

It had slunk over the hoar-frosted field, hunched and hungry, body rigid and bony like a walking carcass, blood-red eyes a-prowl over the vacant property while the cows all huddled unknowingly under the bodark tree. Who'd save the critters under that crass full moon? Would those drunken men over their playing cards, their backward-wheeling chairs? Coyotes yipped in the ravine when she finally turned off the light and prayed to sweet Jesus in her bed, cackling, hunting rabbits, all spackled with shards of November moonlight. Her father and his friends bellowed with laughter, for a moment drowning out all those wild sounds, and when they stopped, the field outside was quiet. She'd seen it, though. She knew.

Next morning, Dad was conked out on the blue corduroy couch. It was Saturday. It was a sunny morning. Janice went to the kitchen and got a glass of water. Mom was sleeping in her parents' bedroom. She went to the living room window, scratching her arm, glad it was Christmas break, only now she was stuck here on this little plot of country land with a werewolf roaming at large, and the night, though far away, would eventually make a comeback. She drank the water and took a quick pee. She went back to her bedroom, which was clotted by a mess of clothes and dolls she would need to clean up that day, and split her checkered curtains. The sunshine made her blink, but then the picture of her world became clear. There was the blue chicken coop in the back yard, just behind the fence, and the rusty old tractor and its plow blade raised above a tangle of jagweed. She had forgotten to close the door of the coop the night before because she was afraid the werewolf might be chasing her, so the hens already pecked at the feed on the ground. Three, four, five, six, seven. . .all accounted for, a miracle. She went outside through the backdoor and crossed the backyard. It was a cold morning, but the sun was warm on her face. She bunched her hands in the pockets of her hoodie, her jaw rigid with vigilance. It was Saturday and Christmas break. It should've been the most wonderful time of the year. The field behind the chicken coop was empty except for a few grazing cattle. They seemed to be okay. They weren't dripping with blood or skittish from the horror of the previous night. The red-brown grass swayed like ocean waves in the brittle morning wind. Janice went through the backyard gate, closed it behind her, and slipped inside the chicken coop. Everything was normal in there. The hay was still all matted and spread across the floor. The sunlight came through the meshed window opening, making little dashes of goldenness on the ground. It smelled like chicken shit, plywood, and dry hay. It was colder here than it was outside.

Well, strange. She didn't know what to make of last night. She still trusted her childish eyesight, though. She had stooped to pick up the eggs in the darkness. She had stepped into the starry night air. She had glanced at the blue-dim horizon with the eggs in the hammock of her smock, and there the werewolf pranced, on the edge of the field. It was like a grisly ghost. It must have been matted with the blood of other schoolchildren. It probably hated Christmas break and everything else good and noble in the world. She remembered. The sun had been setting, yes, and the apricot tones of the sunset had blanketed the open field in something of a haze, a shadow, but the creature was otherworldly, borne from the full moon. Janice spread more chicken feed on the ground. The hens ran to it and devoured it. She found a hole in the chicken-wire fence and used a pair of pliers to mend it shut. She stood up, feeling warmer. A pan clattered in the kitchen sink so loud she could hear it from out here. It was time to go inside. Whether she would speak of the werewolf was still an open question.

She had a history of seeing odd things that others didn't. Everyone sort of knew it, too. A couple of Christmases ago, two of Janice's cousins on her mother's side, Jimmy and Randy, visited for the afternoon. The three of them decided to go to the creek behind the barn out back. The water was frozen solid, so they spent a few minutes sliding around, falling down, laughing, getting red-faced and joyous. Suddenly, something big thrashed through the dry leaves farther up the hill. The cousins were wrestling with each other on the bank and making their own loud noises, but Janice was standing up on the other side of the creek, turned around, and there it was: a black bear lumbering through the trees, alarmed by the unexpected human company.

"A bear, a bear, a bear!" she shouted. When the boys had got up and dusted themselves off, though, it was already gone. They rushed up to look for tracks but found nothing but a trail of disturbed leaves. Another time, when she was by herself, she was fairly certain she found a line of mountain lion prints along the very same creek. She ran back home, dragged Mom out of the house, but halfway out there it started to rain, and they had to turn back to escape the deluge. Janice felt as though the universe was keen on letting her glimpse the dangerous beasts of the world but for some reason wouldn't set her up with any corroborating eyewitnesses. She was the girl who cried wolf.

She went back inside and picked up her book about princesses and dragons and fearsome beasts, which she was halfway through, and settled with it on the couch in the living room while Dad pawed through the kitchen cabinet in search of aspirin. Mom was still clunked out in the bedroom.

Janice looked up from her book. Dad found his aspirin and downed a couple of tablets with a glass of water, wincing, balling up his spare fist at the hem of his rumpled plain white T. The little Shiatzu, Tobie, skittered across the hardwood floor and yapped at the door. Dad looked over and winced again. "Mornin' honey," he said.

"Morning Daddy."

"You're up early."

"It's nine a.m."

Dad belched. "Yup. Early. Your momma still in bed?"

She nodded. Dad pursed his lips and patted the taut paunch of his belly. One too many drinks with the boys. For a moment when his eyes were clasped shut in another yawn, he looked little older than a boy. But really he was thirty-three.

"How's the book?"

"It's all right."

He leaned against the counter and nodded. "Whew," he said, and stretched his nose around with his upper lip. She wanted to talk to him about the werewolf. About its blood-dripping mandibles. About the hellish fairies in the woods on the other side of the creek, those dank sirens beckoning way up in the oaken branches, needling their long white fingers all full of mischief. All that stuff was in her book, vivid and horrifying, way scarier than Harry Potter. Harry Potter was *so* last Christmas.

"Oh man, what a time, Skipper," said Dad. He shook his head. "You want some orange juice? You had anything for breakfast?"

"Not yet."

"Well, dang, kid, here." He poked around the kitchen, got a bowl, messily poured Fruity Pebbles and the last yellow-white layer of skim milk, and brought it over to her on the couch.

"Bon Appetit." He belched again and turned on the TV. "You 'member your mom coming inside last night?"

"Nope. I was asleep."

"Hmm. Gal's a night owl or something."

Janice took a bite of pebbles. On the TV, Oklahoma was playing Georgia in the first round of the College Football Playoff. Early kickoff. *Dad, so, uh, I saw a giant werewolf last night when I was gathering the eggs. Thought you should know.*

She took another bite of cereal and stared at the TV. She knew nothing about football. Dad knew everything about football and always talked over the commentators in ever-increasing volume.

Mom finally walked into the living room, silently, bleary-eyed, her hair done up in a messy bun, dressed in baggy sweatpants and an extra-large hoodie.

She went straight to the kitchen and poured some coffee into a black mug. She winced as well, like Dad had winced, and looked at her husband at the recliner with a slight quiver in her lip. "Are you *kidding* me? How the hell was that not an illegal *block in the back*?" Mom stared at him as she sipped the coffee and leaned her stomach against the edge of the counter. She watched her husband. Her husband watched the TV. Janice watched her mother.

The whole day passed in like fashion, more or less. Mom passed in and out of rooms, never quite snapping out of her bleariness, doing the laundry and snacking in the kitchen, throwing those cold, hungry glances into the living room while Dad enjoyed a full slate of SEC football in front of the tube and Janice made progress on her book. One of the werewolves in the story ended up falling in love with the maiden, only he had to chain himself up at night because otherwise he would murder the girl in her sleep. So, every night at ten p.m., he put the chains on his neck, wrists, and ankles in the basement, turned into a monster, and thrashed against his bondage until morning. Then he would go back to loving the maiden like nothing happened. Janice put the book down and went to find Mom, who was folding underwear in her bedroom and sniffing back her bad sinuses.

"Mom?"

"Huh? What?"

"What're you doing?"

"What's it look like I'm doing, honey."

Janice stood in the doorway. The light was noonday light, now, full-throated yellow light. It fell on Mom's face and made her even paler than she really was.

"I. . .uh. . .well, I think I saw something last night."

Mom looked up and stopped folding laundry. Then she started again and looked back down at the underwear.

"What did you see?"

"Something big. It was covered in black fur and had red eyes. It was in the cow field when I was getting the eggs."

Mom sniffed, said, "Hm!" and grabbed for her water bottle on the nightstand. "Maybe another bear?" She smiled.

"No, don't think it was a bear."

"Huh. Maybe a big old coyote?"

"No. It was bigger than a coyote."

"Wow. Well. Maybe it was a cow. It's hard to see clear at night, you know."

Mom blew her nose into a tissue and bunched up Dad's underwear and tossed it into the top drawer of their shared dresser.

"I'm sorry you were scared, honey," she said. "But I don't think you need to worry about it."

"Do you have to work again tonight?"

"Yeah, baby, I work nights on the weekend, remember?"

Yes, she did remember. Why she needed clarification today, she didn't know. She went back to her silly book and waited for the night to come, for Christmas to come. Well, she did know, actually. She wanted Mom to go out to the coop with her that night to get the eggs. Or Dad. Someone. Anyone.

Mom left for work around seven p.m. and Dad had a couple of the same pals over for the evening around 8 p.m., and by that time it was well past dark and Janice had locked herself away in her bedroom, eggs still uncollected, her lone chore still undone, while Dad and his buddies chortled about the day's football victories and pulled out the alcohol shelf. Mom and Dad had an agreement. He would work on weekdays in construction and fencing and house flipping. She would work at Walgreen's on weekends to help pay off the debt for the new Toyota Camry. They were supposed to do that for six months and then Mom would back off and focus more on her Etsy side gig and taking care of the farm. They were a year into the agreement. Dad wasn't making enough yet for her to switch back to her passion.

Along with the dudes, a woman, no older than 25, walked in behind one of Dad's friends, dressed in a leather jacket, blonde hair done up, red lips and dashing white smile at the ready.

"Brought my girl over, Rob, hope that's all right. This is Molly." Dad gulped down the first beer and nodded, waving her in. "Hell yeah, man, more the merrier!"

The eggs weren't the main concern. Janice needed to go out and close the stupid coop door, and that would take another bold trek through the backyard under the full moon. And her book had ended with the werewolf escaping his bonds and having his maniacal way with the maiden. Just terrible. Why did her parents let her read such awful stuff? They didn't read it first to make sure it was okay—that was why. Janice put her fingers near the red-hot prongs of the heater. She sat against the wood-paneled wall and studied her checkered blinds, the moonlight forcing its patterns into focus. She must save the chickens. They didn't do anything wrong. They deserved better. It was time to be brave and save the chickens, who were dumb but lovable in their innocence.

After she had done the deed, which involved crawling out her window, dropping into the backyard, scooping up the eggs and slamming the door shut without even looking at the horizon on the field, she almost couldn't even believe she'd taken the plunge. But the four beige eggs were in her lap, unbroken, her heart was pounding, and her cheeks were ruby red from the bite of a wicked cold snap, and her window was bolt and shut. She didn't know if the werewolf was back on the prowl. It didn't matter. She was safe for now.

She slipped out of her room and set the eggs in its straw basket on the kitchen counter. Dad, his friends, and the new girl all sat around the round table under a garish light bulb, with the biggest window in the house gaping behind Dad's back. He was unaware of the darkness outside. No one else was looking, either. But Janice saw it. Yes, its mandibles appeared against the shadows of the window, that cold and hungry stare penetrating Dad's unknowing backside, its bleary eyes still waking up from the haunts of the night. The werewolf was there just outside the window, working its late shift, gaping at a domestic scene it would never know. No one saw it except for Janice. But before she could cry wolf, the creature seeped into the blackness, become one with it, and Dad said, "Hey, Skipper! Can you bring us those chips on the counter?"

What else could she do? Janice gave them the chips, petrified anew, and then went back to her room. She lay on her bed and buried her head beneath her pillow. At least her heater still worked. It hummed and warmed her like the mouth of a friendly dog. She thought the werewolf might bust through the window and eat her any minute now, but it didn't, and the minutes passed with ever-increasing levels of peace. The heater murmured in its faithful way, her care bears gazed on her in inanimate love, and she finally fell asleep, her checkered curtains slightly parted, the empty window holding nothing but the full moon in its frame. She slept until the sun shone coldly over the frost-trodden farm.

She woke up before anyone else, same as the morning before, and went into the living room. The dining table was covered in empty Bud Light cans and pizza-smeared paper plates. Right outside the window, where the werewolf had reared its head, the dark branches of the pear tree dipped a little bit in the morning breeze.

The Blockhead

DUSTIN wasn't crazy and had no history of hallucination, but. . .

He woke up the morning before the Christmas mixer with a pair of pillar-shaped blocks for legs, the wooden kind that children play with on living room floors when they're five. The kind they make mock Parthenons out of. The kind they herald heavenward like swords. Now, it was hard for Dustin to prove this to anyone else, since after he stood up, wobbled in just his drawers at the edge of the bed, stiffly limped to the bathroom, and managed to get into his white-collar apparel, his legs reappeared right after he closed his apartment door behind him. Maybe he imagined the blocks? These circular protuberances, paltry substitutes for human legs, turning him into an infertile half-brick, had him a little confused, but he was walking downtown again in no time, and brushed the delusion sideways to focus on the needs of the day: His accounts to manage, his loans to dispense, his coffee to consume, his powerful boss to please, his crush to woo at the Christmas mixer.

He reached the office two minutes before the business day began. All was the same in that glass palace of modules, of invisibly whirring emails going across the void, the HR pleasantries, the rip-roaring laughs of the higher-ups and the bashful go-along chuckles of the newly initiated. Ahh, life. Ahh, the cubicle. Ahh, the acrid bite of corporate coffee on the tongue. Ahh, to have *legs,* to have surely imagined that morning's inexplicable horror! Dustin was still his white-shirted, brown-shoed self, dark hair slicked and trimmed, neck all shaved, golf clubs still stowed in his bedroom corner, the Christmas mixer that night still looming—the mixer where *ohhh Caroline* would almost certainly be in attendance. That is, unless she took that one extra day of accrued PTO and jetted out today instead of Saturday morning. This might be his singular shot to converse with dear Caroline, who snacked on granola two cubicles nigh, stood up with a confident clearing of the throat, adjusted her green Christmas sweater over her hips, and walked with aplomb to the break room to secure her own special caffeine concoction: English tea, almost blacker than Dustin's traditional brew.

All was normal. The phone rang, the emails trickled, the meeting reminders pinged, the blurry glass trim of his cubicle bled with human silhouettes passing by. Ricky stopped by for his morning dose of small talk.

"Well, buddy, here we are. Crazy."

"Yeah, man. Crazy."

"Just crazy."

Dustin didn't ask what in particular was "crazy." For these workplace associates, everything was always crazy year-round for vague reasons no one had the verbal acuity to name but that everyone could nonetheless feel in their inner nodes.

"Already almost Christmas!"

"Crazy."

"Doing anything special for the holidays?" Ricky asked.

Dustin paused. He leaned back in his chair. Was he doing anything special? Dorothy was coming home for Christmas, back in Virginia. Mom and Pops wanted him there, too, obviously; what of Calvin? Who knew. The nomad was last spotted in Yemen, smuggled northward toward the Himalayas. Calving was a photojournalist with a penchant for eastern mysticism. Maybe the youngest of the brood had shed his western affections for the yuletide for good. Dorothy, though. Yes. Sweet big sister Dorothy, practicing law in New York City, friends with everyone of stately import, thirty-three and too gorgeous and rich for marriage, would stoop southward for the annual eggnog.

"Going home, I guess," said Dustin.

"*I'll be home for Christmas. . .*" sang Ricky. His baritone Crosby needed some tinkering, but the heart was there. He almost went on with the song but must have realized he didn't know any of the other lyrics. He cleared his throat and clapped his fist against his alternate palm.

"Well, son, you going to the Christmas mixer? The company mixer? Whatever it is? Tonight?"

"Sure, I'll be there."

"Hey, hey." Ricky flicked Dustin on the shoulder and winked toward Caroline's empty cubicle. "Shoot your shot, dawg. I'm your wing man." He upheld his ring finger. "I've been through the ringer, buddy. Wouldn't go back through the meat grinder of modern dating ever again. No sir. Monogamy for me. Understand?"

Dustin grinned and nodded. "I think so. No rush, though, right?"

"That's what they all say. 'No rush.' Huh!"

Caroline emerged from the break room, stirring her tea intently as she dealt with the fractious balance of her pair of high heels. Luckily, this meant she would take longer than usual to voyage over the office floor. So, Ricky was obliged to continue his hard-earned wisdom.

"When Lily and I met, I was a platypus. Literally, dawg. Flippers for hands. Oblong as a flattened skittle. Pardon the graphic metaphors. Just trying to be concrete here. I was a creative writing major in college. Track with me? But here's the rub. We got to talking. I got to looking at her sea-green eyes. I got to hearing about her travails at NYU. I got to listening to her talk about her horse Bucky back in Tennessee. How this gal really wanted the simplicity of a good old country life but here she was in the Big Apple, tensioned like a rubber band. I got to be interested in *her*, dawg. Platypus features slowly dissolved. I became human again. Self-consciousness utterly abandoned. I *saw*. Eventually, I *loved*."

Maybe Ricky's skill in sagacious deliveries were unique to the holiday season, but Dustin nodded along, impressed, and considered the merit of Ricky's words off and on for the rest of day. The thing was, he had never, you know, *spoken* to Caroline. They were the same age, more or less, both graduates of Colombia. The intellects would be comparable. Both financiers at the same firm, the salaries would be comparable. Both in their late twenties and still beauteous in the bloom of youth, the intimacy would be rapturous, surely. Who *was* she, though? Beyond the cubicle, beyond the slight smiles she proffered when he passed her in the corridors, brief meetings that rendered him into a puddle the moment they ended?

"Yes, you're going to the mixer. Excited for it. And remember. You're *talking* to her. Like a man, damn it. Understand?"

"Yeah, Ricky. I get it. Thanks, man."

She was back at her cubicle and that night's mixer was a fast-approaching mountain. He would soon be asked to climb it.

Dustin didn't bother to go home after the workday ended. And it wasn't because he was scared his legs would turn into blocks. Or so he told himself, at least. He shoved the memory out of his mind, told the mental image of those childish wooden pillar blocks to go down an alley and holler "fish" He dreamed it. That was that. It was the tail-end of a weirdo dream sent to him from an alternative dimension. Or something. He didn't go home, he reasoned, because he simply didn't have the time. He had finished up his calls for the long weekend. Christmas Eve was on Monday, Christmas on Tuesday, so they would have a lucky four-day break this year. He wandered to the coffee shop at the end of the street and ordered a mocha latte, a Friday treat, a Christmas prize. He needed occasional, sweet rewards for his job. It was his dream job, to be clear, but a dream job he hated, to be even clearer. That's not a contradiction. It's the American paradox, infinitely complex. He nodded to himself at the notion. That was work, right? When you finish college, you don't go back home to Virginia and work as a manager at your father's mid-sized paper mill. You don't go back to the bland limits that forged you, threatened to imprison you for life. No, you move to Manhattan and run with the big dogs.

You smite your ancestry with the green dollar and stand on top of the peak looking over the misty mountains. Dustin slicked his raven-black hair back and reclined in the comfy leather chair by the window, watching the people pass by on the sidewalk.

Who should walk in as he checked his watch and rose to his feet but the woman of the hour herself. Young Caroline flipped her brown hair over the back of her collar and adjusted her coat as she sauntered up to the counter, studying the menu. She didn't look around the coffee shop in the meantime, so she didn't notice Dustin sitting by the window as he stood up. She must have had the same idea as he. Get a coffee before the mixer and all of its stresses. Maybe now they would get coffee and then walk to the Christmas mixer back at headquarters, where a catered buffet of roast beef, turkey, dressing, rolls, and wine awaited.

She ordered hot chocolate. He was surprised. He had pegged her for an evening espresso type of lass. Always alert. Always on the verge of burnout. But no. She took the hot chocolate and ambled over to the window on the other side of the room and looked upward at the pinnacles of the city's tallest skyscrapers. She sipped. She cupped her hands around the cup and bowed her head, like a Madonna statue in some church cemetery. When she turned around, Dustin raised his coffee cup.

"Oh, hey there. Dustin, right?"

"Yep, that's me. Caroline, right?" Ah, young love in the age of the internet. Both feigning ignorance after each googling the other in their respective cubicles.

"You going to the party?" said Caroline.

"That was the plan. Decided to get a coffee beforehand."

"Great minds think alike. Only. . ." She pointed to the label on her paper cup. "I went nostalgic today. Something about a hot chocolate sounded good for some reason."

"'Tis the season."

"Well. Shall we walk together?"

"To the party?"

She checked her Apple watch. "Did you have something else in mind beforehand?"

"Huh? Oh!" He blossomed red. "No. I mean. There's no time. Right? What time is it?"

"Quarter 'til seven."

"Then no, we don't have time, that is, no time except for getting to the party. The mixer. Hehe."

Despite his idiotic flop, Caroline laughed, and they walked out into the sub-thirty city air together.

"Any plans for Christmas?" he said.

She shrugged. "Jersey. That's home for me."

"Oh, okay. Jersey's all right."

She shrugged again.

They entered the party together but didn't stay united for long. Caroline veered to connect with a couple of her cubicle comrades, Jill and Tera, and Dustin pulled up to the punch bowl and ladled himself some spirit.

"Well," said Ricky, appearing like an apparition behind his shoulder. "What's happening?"

"Just getting something to drink. Nothing too groundbreaking, here."

"You walked in with her!"

"Pure coincidence."

"You met up beforehand!"

"An honest to God accident, I assure you."

"No accidents in my book, buddy. Only *opportunities.*"

Oh boy. He was about to proverbialize again. Dustin swigged and winced at the tart blast of the punch. Good punch. Ricky, though, only threw his arm around Dustin's shoulder and filled up his own plastic glass with elixir on the festively decorated table. "Just don't be a blockhead. Definition of a blockhead? In my book, it's this: A self-conscious dweeb who lacks the ability to see beyond his own oaken forehead. Savvy?

Dustin raised his glass. Don't be a blockhead. Even when you have blocks for legs.

In retrospect, Dustin didn't even recall exactly how it happened how, after eating his Christmas dinner at Caroline's corner of the party, and chatting with her again at the dessert table, they were on the streets heading back to his apartment at eight p.m., tipsy but far from drunk, in overall festive Christmas spirits. Ricky had given him the knowing eye as they walked out the door together. The long Christmas weekend was before him. He would drive home to Virginia on Sunday. But first, he was going to sleep with sweet Caroline and wake up with her curled on her side in the cold city light.

He reached for his keys and Caroline squeezed the back of his arm. It was actually happening. All those months of daydreams materializing. He opened the door and stepped in. Tea first? More conversation? She had told him about her experience at Colombia, how she actually wanted to be a journalist but had family connections in the finance biz. But someday, you know, she'd like to return to her original fancies and cover the stories of real people, living real lives.

Dustin felt like he had done everything Ricky told him to do. Pay attention. Ask questions. Don't talk about yourself, whatever you do! He felt like he earned the fruits of his labor. He finagled his way through all of the obstructing hoops leading to intimacy, to this point, to sex. However, the second he stepped into his apartment, he almost fell down, had to grip the edge of the kitchen counter to stop the plummet, and when he straightened up, became so pale and wide-eyed that Caroline was already fumbling for her phone to call an ambulance.

"Nonsense!" said Dustin, spinning around and leaning against the counter. "Just tripped. All good!"

He wasn't, of course, "all good." His legs had turned back into wooden pillars the second he crossed the apartment threshold.

As a boy, back in Virginia, he once opened a box of building blocks on Christmas morning and soon constructed a castle, a city, a bridge, a network of highways. He didn't want to ever see it fall. His parents let him keep the civilization intact for a couple of weeks after Christmas but hosted a party at their house in mid-January and tragically had to take the blocks down and relocate the blocks to Dustin's bedroom.

He lamented the loss of his kingdom but used the night to build it all back in his room, and in a more glorious form, so that by the end of the party the long rectangles, squares, curved connectors, ramps, and pillars, were all reunited and in the semblance of a whole. Something unified. Harmonious. His. If he had tried to use his arm as a bridge or his toes for a bulwark, the whole city would be disjointed, unsettled, built on shaky ground. What was God playing on him now? At the moment of connection with the greatest girl north of the Potomac, he was inanimate waist down.

"I'm sorry," he said. "Just sort of lost my balance. Do you want any tea? Coffee?"

Caroline took her coat off, looking concerned as she hung it on the peg on the door. "No thanks. Are you sure you're all right?"

"Perfect!" Dustin tottered to the fridge and managed to open it up and steal a Coors. "Might just be the workout routine I've been on. A real killer."

"Ah. Roughleg day?"

"You could say that."

He didn't know what to do, what excuse to make, what semi-human walking gait to assume on his way to the couch in the living room. He tried to resist the impulse to call an ambulance himself. What would they say when they put him on the gurney with his peg legs in full view only to watch them vanish back into body parts the second they hit the hallway? Wizardry and witchcraft! Maybe he should cancel his lease and move. Where would he go? Virginia? To a rural homestead where a man isn't so divided and doesn't need the lesson to be personified by getting a couple of blocks instead of locomotive hamstrings? He was *born* for the city! He was *born* for this job! He was *born* for this wondrous woman of Columbia cloth.

"Looks like you got some gnarly cramps. Do you need some water?" asked Caroline.

"No! That's okay. It'll pass." He collapsed into the sofa and propped his blocks up on the coffee table. Caroline warily approached him in her black blouse, arms crossed, and sat down next to him just a couple inches beyond kissing range.

"Well," said Dustin. He remembered the words of the wise Ricky. "How do you like your job?"

He was scared his wooden ankles might be exposed, but luckily his pant legs and reindeer fuzzy socks sustained the illusion, and Caroline, far from giving an awkward response, replied that she liked the job all right, but that she missed her hometown, was struggling to make friends in the city, and wanted to teach English somewhere overseas. Dustin nodded. He put the beer on the coffee table and folded his arms. It would be a pretty big change, but she didn't care. She wanted to do something that helped people. She had a brother who lived in Fort Worth, Texas. He sold real estate and was an adjunct professor of business at Texas Christian University. She had an uncle who sadly died in a construction accident seven years prior, and a father who, while he was historically a cheery man, had never seemed to get over his brother's death. She had a mother who worked at a pharmacy and three cousins who were still in college—two at Villanova and another at Penn State. Was she inching closer within range the longer she talked? Strangely, the young man on the couch forgot to notice such physical advances. Those eyes, a rich, caramel brown, strewn with flecks of golden green, a happy laugh that shocked Dustin with its almost childish authenticity, and his own unexpected fear about what that kind of laughter *meant*, made billowing clouds of invisible connection between the two of them. He was so doggone immersed that, yes, he forgot that he had blocks for legs. He forgot even at the door of the apartment three hours later when Caroline got up to leave and said she had to catch a flight early the next morning. Going home for the holidays.

"Call me when you get back, maybe," said Caroline. She kissed him on the cheek and left him standing there in the light-sullied kitchen, his hand resting on the surface of the door. He went to the window. Dark skyscrapers, lower rims adorned with gold, green, and red, shaped her brisk image as she walked down the avenue and melded into the film of partygoers. Ricky called.

"Well?"

"Well what, Ricky?"

"Were you a blockhead?"

"I don't think so. No, in fact. Shockingly, I wasn't."

"And you talked to her? You paid real attention to her face and not her breasts?"

"Yeah, I guess I did."

"How about that. I'm proud. A real proud uncle is what I am." Ricky yawned. "All right. See ya next week."

Ricky hung up the phone and Dustin went back to the living room to fetch the Coors, which was still brimming, gone undrunk. He knitted his brows. Was her presence so powerful that he didn't even care that he merely was half a man? He sat down on the couch and picked up the beer. Goodness gracious. His knees bent and his shoes, all full of real feet, settled on the hardwood floor. Restored after disassembly.

Part II

What the Tree Saw

Many years ago, the old oak tree saw the heavy snowfall of 1855. Snow crowned its branches and buried its trunk in white. Jackrabbits, big as hound dogs, danced through the snow in ones and twos. A stately barred owl frowned from a nook in a nearby elm. A gray fox sniffed after the rabbits and chased a field mouse that tunneled through the snow.

In 1862, a young man in a gray cap and uniform crawled to the base of the tree clutching his stomach and whimpering, "Help me," over and over. His stomach bled into the grass at the foot of the tree and even marked one of the visible roots with red. The soldier sat up against the tree as he moaned, prayed, begged, and bled out. He could not have been more than twenty years old. Shots crackled off somewhere to the south. A couple of musket bullets grazed the tree's top branches. The young soldier, though, kept safe from any more harm until he died later that evening, legs spread, head lolling, and the tattered cloth on his stomach black from dry blood. The tree could not guess what the boy had died for.

Ten years later, a young boy trotted through the forest and paused to look at the skeleton in its tattered military regalia at the foot of the tree. He stooped to get a better look, whooped in terror, and fled back to familiar territory.

In 1901, a group of white men, each holding terrible torches, dragged a black youth to the foot of the tree. They hanged him like they would hang a common criminal, although all he'd done was tip his hat to a white woman who had passed him on the sidewalk in the nearby village. The knot tightened around the innocent man's neck, the bare feet kicked, and the dark ecstasy shone in the mobsters' eyes; long after everyone had left, the lone body gently swayed in the moonlight.

The young man's mother and father found their son and the tree the next morning, bent down at the roots, and wailed. They got him down and carried him back through the woods. The tree felt the young man's weight on its branches for a long, long time afterward.

The tree saw no one, man, woman, or child for seventeen years.

A young man and young woman ran giggling to the foot of the tree and lay out a picnic blanket at its grassy base. They ate biscuits, pickles, and apples. They talked about the weather, the beauty of the forest, and the future. The young man's right ear was missing. The girl didn't seem to mind. She said that they could build a new life together. They could start a family. Be like normal people.

"What'll your father say?"

"He'll come around! And anyway, you'll find a job."

"I promise I will. For us."

They kissed and fell asleep on the picnic blanket, feet touching the green grass at the edge of the cloth.

The man and woman visited their new spot by the tree almost every week for the next year. Every time, the young man looked more subdued, gloomy. The woman asked him what was wrong, reminded him that he'd gotten a good job, that her father liked him all right, that they were building what they wanted to build. The young man would only poke at the ground with a stick and scratch his missing ear. Was he remembering something? Something he could never forget? Hearing something he could never unhear?

One day, in the fall, the man kicked through the leaves all the way to the foot of the tree and put his hand on the trunk.

"Tree," he said. "What can I do? God above! What must I do to be *free*?"

Thirty years later, the trees around the big post oak were leveled and replaced with a belt of fresh interstate. Cars cruised by. The occasional trucker would stop on the shoulder to rest. One time, a big guy from the Bronx, transporting a bunch of logs, took a leak behind the tree and smoked a cigarette.

Ten years after that, a gas station sprouted just a few yards away from the tree. People would stop in their cars, fill up, get snacks, and smoke by the pumps. Kids ran in circles around their family caravans until their mothers scooped them up and plopped them in back seats. The tree saw old ladies dusted in talcum, fresh for Sunday services. It saw little boys in starchy knickers and stiff collars, little girls in pastel blue and pink dresses and white ballerina-like shoes. It saw a tornado totter and rage and pick up the gas station like a thimble in May of 1985. The tree, though, kept standing.

The tree was home to a prodigious home of squirrels from 1990–994, but after the gas station was rebuilt along with the casino, hotel, and food court, most of the old family of animals retreated southward into the untouched sections of the forest. The interstate was almost always busy, even late at night. The tree now lived at the tip of the sword, right against where they'd stopped their industrial blades and tractors.

In 2023, a land surveyor in a yellow hat and yellow vest brought instruments, stakes, and string out near the old oak tree and plotted property points. He made a phone call and then took out a lunch pail. He ate a sandwich and a tangerine while sitting up against the oak tree.

"You're old, aren't you?" he said, knocking a fist against the trunk. "Kind of a shame. Hate seeing big trees go down." He chewed, swallowed, and added, "I wonder what all you've seen in your life, buddy."

The tree was turned into a wealthy woman's table in a Manhattan high rise apartment in the snowy winter of 2025. But now it could no longer see its surroundings and was to be eaten upon by modern men and women. Someday, maybe, it would become a bench on a porch where honeymooning couples would sit, facing the mountains and the next big snow.

Success Story

2,593 videos received on Tuesday, December 3.

4,566 videos received on Friday, December 6.

1,390 videos received on Saturday, December 7.

3.2 million subscribers accrued as of December 8.

It was cold outside, caked with week-old crusts of snow on the roads and sidewalks and front yards. People lost balance and fell down on college campuses. Fat men slipped on back porches, recorded through security cameras, and nursed sprained ankles in an inch of snow with the backyard hound sniffing at their haunches, shirt all hiked up, exposing a little bit of flesh. A woman hoisted up a Christmas tree, lost her balance, and tumbled backwards in a pool of pine nettle and paper stars on little sticks.

To call Tom's "job" stupid might be to state the obvious, but even the critics of internet slop, AI and otherwise, had to admit that even they sometimes sat on the pot after a long day at work and watched TomFoolery and Failure, chuckled at the falls, the groans, the litanies of bleeped out profanity, the tragi-comic sight of seeing a human being temporarily helpless, beaten by nature, under the weather of the world.

Tom started his account when he was 20 years old and five years later enjoyed a full-time job as a curator of the modern world's biggest and funniest failures captured on camera. Yes, he had competitors in the industry, and certain pirate accounts that swiped his content, but for now, he was top dog. People sent him hundreds, nay, thousands of videos every single day of the year. Content spiked on holidays, especially the Fourth of July. Drunk fails can be wild, man. Too wild. *Every* day of the year, though, parents sent videos of their kids. Coworkers sent videos of their bosses. Son-in-law betrayed father-in-law and daughter betrayed mother. And if all these videos just represented the fails that were caught on camera, just imagine how many times human beings fell in the mud every single day, every single minute. Talk about job security.

Tom lived with a heavy gamer and streamer named Gary, or G-Money-Gamer-Gary-Demon-Slayer depending on the app, on the second floor of a new apartment complex on the south side of the city. The little surrounding village was part of a new community project intended mainly for young singles and newly budded families who wanted a middle-ground between fast-paced downtown and boring suburbia. Although designed to "foster" community and family, built with a little town square in the middle with a walkable web of sidewalks and bridgework, togetherness still felt hard to come by.

Tom walked every afternoon to a coffee shop on the corner of Turner and Houston. On his way, every day, he passed by a long building, taking up half a block, with an empty first-floor ballroom stretched behind clear glass windows. The building had been for sale for months, and Tom even floated the idea of buying it and creating that multimedia conglomerate he'd always dreamed of. But no. On that crisp day in mid-December, his scarf wrapped tightly below his golden curls of youth, Tom passed a newly purchased first-floor ballroom, one that was filled not with people in suits and computer screens but a bunch of little kids climbing on a jungle of indoor playground equipment. He happened to be on the other side of the street but still stopped for a second to look. There were around 20 kids in the play place, all ten years old or younger, dressed in their Saturday shorts and tennis shoes, running all around the turf yard and over the rubber mounds, crawling through plastic tunnels, screaming loud enough to deafen armies. Parents stood nearby, snapping pictures, chatting with each other with eye rolls and laughter. Many of them filmed their children with their iPhones. Soon, one small girl put her arms above her head and spun around on her tippy toes on top of a rubber mound only to tumble backwards into a pool of her own dress, feet straight up in the air. That was fail video material if Tom had ever seen any.

Kids tripped and wailed. One of them knocked a bystanding adult right off her feet, making her drop her cappuccino. But they were, without a doubt, having *fun*, the unselfconscious kind of fun that's hard not to smile at when you're old and jaded and numb. They kept falling, getting back up, falling, getting back up.

Tom moved on from the site and ordered his usual coffee with a smile and a one-dollar tip. He didn't stop by the play place on his way back. It was too cold to give it another glance, a brash draft of wind was throwing his scarf backward, and he needed to check his email for that week's curation of film.

A few minutes after Tom had walked back to his apartment, the same girl got on top of that pesky rubber mound, spun in a circle, and kept her balance for the rest of the hour she had left to play. Her mom even got a video of the success story, but sent it only to her husband, who smiled at it during a business meeting in Dubai.

I've Lost My Way, Macy

"I feel like, I don't know, like I've lost my way, Macy."

"Sounds dramatic." She eats away at her ice cream cone. Stars shimmer above the oak boughs. The lake is a black palm shivering in the breeze.

"I'm serious. I don't know what the heck I'm doing."

Slurp, chuckle.

"What's gotten into you?"

"*Life* has gotten into me. I didn't think I'd be here ten years ago. Didn't think all I'd be doing is driving trucks for a living."

Okay. That merits a lowering of the ice cream cone and a glance away from the romantic stars and a glare into Ryan's face.

"You're not happy with where you're at? You're not happy that you're with me?"

"That's not what I meant."

"Sounds like it's what you meant."

"It's not." Ryan swallows and presses his ball cap over his brow and asks, lamely, "How's the ice cream?"

"It's cold, Ryan. Cold and clammy. I don't know. I thought we were having a nice night."

"We are having a nice night. I just wanna talk. I'm trying to talk."

"Well. This isn't how I thought we were going to talk."

People in relationships, if you're like Macy and Ryan, meet each other at a country bar in Ardmore and then get to know each other in Macy's trailer house on the edge of town. And they venture to hike in the foothills to prove they can date like fancy people. Dip their heads into the waterfall and everything. Hold hands on the forest path and everything. Did he ever tell he loved her? That's the kind of honesty she wants from him. She doesn't want him to tell her he's falling apart like some child without a mother. She doesn't want a guy who is on the verge of a breakdown, who has the calloused hands of a trucker, an oil rigger, a cowboy, an everything. What's she to do with tenderness? It's confounding. It's unromantic.

"I don't know how to talk very good."

"It ain't hard. Why don't you tell me something good? Something you like about me?"

"I do tell you things I like about you."

"I don't know if you do." She goes back to the ice cream but lets it fall upside down so the remaining scoop plummets into the leaves in a pink sludge. Strawberry. A little too sweet for his taste. She nibbles at the cone and soon gives up on that, too. Ryan didn't get any ice cream. He is having an existential crisis and can't stomach dessert. Feels sort of disrespectful to the gravity of the moment, like ice cream would just ruin the one time in his life he feels this way, like a cattail reed bending with the wind, vulnerable to snap. Can he give an honest account about his sudden flirt with vulnerability? All he can figure is that two days ago he was driving across the flatlands of west Texas, and he turned the radio off, and he turned his phone off, and he was driving across a whole bunch of beautiful nothingness with just his lonesome thoughts, thinking first about Macy, then about this job, then about how he missed his sister, and how his sister always used to tell him to go be an astronaut and learn to fly spaceships and to leave this little town but to not forget her when he was famous. And about how his sister laughed at his bad jokes when nobody else did and how she didn't deserve to die like that, how nobody, let alone a nice girl like his sister, deserves to die like that. *Jesus,* he had prayed in the silence. *This is why I listen to the damn radio. To get away from this.*

How to talk to Macy about it? How to discuss the feeling that he's lost his way in the world? Maybe he had no "way" in the first place and he's just sort of been mucking around in all these different swamps for his whole life. Working oil rigs. Cowboying up near Stillwater. Now this, trucking all over the southwest, sleeping on a cot in the backseat of his semi-truck, taking Macy, a divorcee at 23, to get strawberry ice cream at Braum's on a Tuesday night.

"Tell me you want me," she says.

"I want you."

"Do you really?"

"I just said it, didn't I?"

"Only 'cause I asked you, too." But she's guilty for her mind tricks and adds, "I don't think you're off your rocker. Ain't nobody perfect. You're on the right path. Don't know what it is that makes you think otherwise. I don't mind being with a trucker. Been with a lot worse, I can tell you that much."

He shakes his head and takes his hat off to wipe his sweating forehead. "I don't know why I said that. It ain't nothing, really. I guess I just. . .I don't know. Was driving the other day and shut off the noise. Started really missing Amy. That was my sister. I ain't told you about her. I don't talk about her."

Now Macy is chafed with regret and bites her lower lip and doesn't know what to say, because there isn't anything to say, and that's okay sometimes. It really is.

"She, uh. Well. She died when we was kids. Just an accident, you know. Daddy had her on his lap on the tractor. Hit a bump, she falls off. She was thirteen years old. Too big to be sitting on Daddy's lap. But she wanted to. She wanted to be with him. She couldn't be apart from him. Begged to go with him. And I told her that she was too old for that. And I was only ten at the time. Already being an idiot trying to tell her what to do, how to feel. She just loved her daddy. That's all. That's all she was guilty of."

Macy can say nothing in response to him. She can only wonder at all the things people hide from each other, and maybe for good reason, seeing how very few people on earth can bear to hear the pain in someone else's voice. Or know how to retranslate it into normalcy. Even the voices of people they love.

"C'mon," Ryan said, patting her knee. "This is sad stuff. I want some ice cream, too."

The Highway of Brightness

A red, 1975 Ford F-150 rolled into Hank's Gas and Bite-To-Go on the last day of the establishment's existence. Hank, now eighty, swiveled on a stool behind the counter as he puffed on his sixth cigarette of the day, having counted all the money and put it in his leather zip-up pouch. He was staring from time to time down the black belt of empty highway bounding up and down the white-capped buttes, as though he expected the grim reaper to show up and call his number. Instead, the red truck chugged up to the station, parked next to the pumps, and stopped, engine puffing fumes into the December air. Hank stood up and leaned against the counter. He craned his neck over the plastic baked goods container and scratched his chest. No one got out of the truck. The driver's head wasn't visible from Hank's point of view. Well? Was the man going to gas up or what?

A vicious gust of Wyoming wind made the structure sing in its creases, and the old man wrapped his leather coat tighter around his shoulders. He had had no customers since last Tuesday. Before they built the interstate thirty miles north, people came in and out of the station year-round, even in winters like these. Back then, he hired college kids in the summers. His wife Penny, who died five years earlier, God bless her soul, made dream catchers and wooden figurines and even jackknifes to sell in the shop. This whole gas station thing was her idea after his business ventures in

Denver didn't pan out. "Can't always pick your road trips," she told him. "Let's plant here for a while."

Now, cars drove by only when the interstate was being snowplowed, or when the occasional soul preferred a more scenic route, as if Wyoming wasn't scenic all around. For about ten years during the station's golden age, another married couple worked for him full-time. Times change, though, and Hank was old. Most of his friends had either already died or retired in Denver, and he was due to move into an old folks' home in Cheyenne per his only daughter Judy's arrangement. Judy had visited him a month ago and finally convinced him to hang up the keys and condemn the ancient convenient store. It was to be an empty husk on the highway shoulder until the elements beat it down to selfsame gravel and flotsam. She was coming back later that afternoon with a U-Haul to help him make the trip south. That was kind of her. She was all he really had left at that point.

Hank stood up, cracked his knuckles, and then stifled the cigarette on the glass counter. The red truck still stood there in the lot, unmoving, with no one stepping out to gas up or grab a quick bite to go. Hank leaned against the door and grimaced from the brackish light that poured through the glass window. It was so bright outside, as if the winter had bartered with the sun to let its pale rays get a share of atmosphere. But he felt like in all his forty years manning the store that it had never been colder. He was right. It hadn't. The temperature gauge on the wall outside the door read—17.

Maybe the driver was simply checking his map, needing to redirect himself to the interstate and get back on his merry way. Maybe she was a woman, Wyoming bred and born, and was eating a sandwich in the warmth of the truck.

Hank took a bag of beef jerky, the last one on the rack, and munched as he watched. Five minutes passed. Ten. Still the red truck puffed and hummed in its place. Had he seen this vehicle before? Something about its glossy sheen, the sleek metal bumper, clear glass, old black tires not even barely scuffed with snow gunk, made him think that maybe he had. He snapped his fingers. He had seen such a truck once in Seattle, chugging up a steep hill a half mile away from his father's funeral back in 1975. He didn't know why he watched it climb the residential mountain from the steps of the cathedral, while the mourners all touched his shoulder, whispering condolences. But he had, until the truck topped the hill and vanished. Now the same brand of red sleigh was parked in the brightness of the Bite-to-Go, and still no pilot emerged from the cockpit.

Hank got his gloves on and Pendleton winter cap on and stepped into the tundra. It took only a couple of steps at an angle for him to realize there was no driver in the truck at all and given that the scene had at least flitted in his periphery for the past twenty minutes, he had no clue where the culprit might be. A silver key was stuck in the ignition, winking with sunlight. An old Dakota blue blanket lay folded on the passenger seat, and a green thermos set in the cupholder, lid open, steaming with coffee. Hank stepped away from the truck, frowning, and dared to look beneath the truck. There was nothing except for empty Coca-Cola can bottle that rolled over the concrete all the way to the edge of the empty lot.

"Hello?" he called out. He walked around the gas station, poked around the dump, and stroked his neck scruff on the way back around, feeling a little bit haunted. He went back in the station and repeated, "Hello?" Nothing. Either the driver had sprinted into the foothills or else was seated beneath a cloak of invisibility in the front seat. It was about noon but seemed like it had been such for hours at that point, with the open sky and its diamond sun blinding him and filling the windows with glare. He didn't know what to do. Judy might be there any minute. How was he supposed to explain an empty red truck in the lot, still running? Hank paused his ruminations and sipped the last of his cold cup of coffee. His own car, a broken-down Toyota Highlander, was in mid-repair behind the station. He had no interest, really, in dying in a lonely nursing home in Cheyenne, feebly inching down felt-carpet hallways in a walker with nothing to look forward to except a short Sunday visit from Judy. He could not drive West in the old

Highlander, but what about the red truck, gleaming even brighter by the gas pump, nearly asking for a new captain to guide her down that abandoned highway to some final, unknown destination? Old Hank, who had not so much as stolen a gumball in his life, felt his legs propel back into the cold, and without even thinking it over again, pulled himself into the truck's warm interior. He sniffed the coffee thermos and took a small sip. It was good coffee. He took another drink and reached down to put the beauty into gear. He had to jolt back, though, when the gear knob readjusted into first, second, third, and fourth on its own volition. He couldn't bail now. The truck had already veered onto the highway and reached a comfortable sixty miles per hour.

"Sometimes," a woman's voice on the radio said, softly, "you can't pick your road trips. You gotta let God do the driving. Well, that's okay. It's good, in fact. I'll be here with you every mile in the brightness, until you to wherever it is you're going to. Plant here a while, won't you?"

It was his dead wife's voice, then it was everyone's voice, then it was all light and a song—"Buddy"—by Willie Nelson, surrounding him and that empty West-bound road.

It was fitting, then, when Judy walked into Hank's Gas and Bite-to-Go later that day and found her father slumped against the glass window on his old stool, his eyes still trained on the long stretch of the bright, black highway, waiting for her.

Part III

Touch Air

I *want* to want something besides this screen and this dank, book-lined room. To touch air. A human face. But my mind caterwauls, get blocked up by pusillanimity, gets too self-conscious for transcendence. Back to the page and its mockery, its bright edges of possibility.

Once, I pulled out of the parking lot behind my college apartment and a bunch of red autumn leaves fluttered across the windshield like happy throwing stars. "I Am Easy to Find" by The National played through the speakers. "I'm not going anywhere," Matt Berninger sang alongside the murmurs of an unknown woman. "Who do I think I'm kidding?"

For a second, I was shown that life, at its bone basis, is good. It amounted to one glimpse of glory, a half-spoon measured modicum of eternity, and I've been looking for it ever since. As if squinting my eyes or getting binoculars is supposed to help me find "it." It's old news that God hides everywhere.

The Shape Shifter

The Shape Shifter packages landed on doorsteps in the city of Vent on a peachy Saturday morning. All up and down Free Street, where the houses were all straight as corn stalks, painted friendly pastel colors with gables carved like wedding cakes, residents stepped on their patios, phones in hand, and snuck their packages into their foyers. One of these residents was a thirty-year-old man named Hamish Johnson, and like everyone else on Free Street in Vent, he worked from home, spoke to no one, and was among the first to buy this new contraption of wonder. Hamish set the box on his table and marveled at how small it was. He got out a kitchen knife and slit the tape from the top of the box and then stepped away as if the object inside might pounce. It didn't, of course. It did, however, assume a humanoid form. Hamish folded back the cardboard and read the instructions: "Calibrate Shape Shifter to imitate any style, character, orientation, shape, and predisposition you prefer! Test out what kind of romantic partners and friends you like best with Shape Shifter!" Simple enough. He wanted someone like Michelle; he knew that much. Could he, though, remember what she truly looked like? The Shape Shifter stood to its full height now and in its innocent, glassy form with a blank screen on its chest waiting for initiation. "Can you hear me?" said Hamish.

"I compute," replied the Shape Shifter. "But before you begin, a disclosure from Open Skies Incorporated: A Shape Shifter is a robotic entity. It cannot and *should* not be confused with a human person. Do you understand?"

"I understand," said Hamish, a little sheepish at the question.

"In that case," the Shifter said, "hello, neighbor!"

Backspace

Jake C. Cloverfeld | Sales Assistant at Limelight Health and Fitness | Positivity and Leadership | Building a Healthier World.

Backspace. Jake taps the keyboard, drinks a dose of his coffee, and peers over the cubicle. Backspace.

Jake C. Cloverfeld | Sales Associate at Limelight Health and Fitness | Positivity and Self-Optimization | Striving for a Healthier World.

Backspace. Backspace.

The profile picture stares back at him in its professional attire, its overly white smile, its gelled hair and tanned cheekbones. It taunts him as if it's someone else, like a cat's reflection taunts its owner in the mirror, makes it play with itself endlessly. *Is that you?* it says. *Are you me?*

Backspace.

Jake C. Cloverfeld | Husband | Father | Community Builder | Striving for a Healthier Planet | Equity and Care for All | Buy Fitness Package Below!

Ahem. You've exceeded the limit. Backspace. . .

A colleague walks by and glances at the open LinkedIn profile page on the computer screen. He lightly laughs, and chimes, "How's the first day, Jake?"

"Hey! It's good, man, good!"

Backspace.

Jake C. Cloverfeld | Sales Associate at Limelight Health and Fitness.

Ready to publish? Is that *all* you are?

Jake C. Cloverfeld hits "publish" so as to mark the completion of a major life update and rises to refill his coffee cup. He has to meet everyone in the conference room in thirty minutes. Thirty minutes is enough time to craft a compelling introduction and brand himself and adopt various corporate identities. A statement of purpose. That's what the leadership wants from him. A nutshell version of himself. He fills up his coffee, returns to his cubicle, and opens up his profile page. He sighs.

Backspace.

Moses on the Mountain

Moses sat on the mountain, eyes closed, his hands folded on his lap.

God said, "Don't peek, or you'll die."

Moses said, "Yes, Lord."

God ruffled his robes and spun in the air and laughed, but the laughter sounded like evil thunder to Moses's ears and blew the Hebrew on the ground at the foot of his little rock.

"Ah! Poor man," said God.

"For a day I hiked up the mountain to glimpse Thine holiness, but now that I have arrived, I can't bring myself to bend mine eye upon Thee, not even Thy backside!" cried Moses.

Moses expected thunder and cracked stone and smoke from the mountain's zenith, volcanic and heavy and holy. But things fell quiet on the mountain instead. Globs of sunlight broke through the clouds of justice and trio of desert jays chattered in a nearby olive tree, which Moses hadn't noticed before.

"Lord?"

All he got in reply, though, were the birds, which bounced from bough to bough, streaks of purple and brown feathers fiery with the light. Moses held his little horns in fear. "I am vexed. Did Thou not promise, Lord, to pass over me and show me Thy backside?"

When the tree crackled with clear fire, and the desert birds melded into the singular flame, Moses did not, now, cower. Nay, he *looked.*

"Remember me?" said God.

My Roommate is a Walrus with Whiskers

My roommate is a walrus with whiskers and white glasses. He sits, nay, he *lounges* by the window, washed over with gaunt morning light, a flipper holding up classic literature, be it *Moby Dick, Don Quixote,* or *Hamlet,* and thumbs through the pages with a downturned lip, great obtrusive tusks almost brushing the hardwood floors. Sir Walrus is an *intellectual* although no one knows how he makes money; we shouldn't ask, because he pays rent from a deep pocket, recites poetry in his sleep, and waddles to the park to feed the pigeons every Saturday. He is not a mobster. He is not a conman. He is a decent, respectable citizen and creature of letters.

I don't ask questions, I don't jab the flab, I don't call local authorities. I have a walrus for a roommate. It's just a fact of existence. Isn't life wonderful?

Open Windows

THE window is open when Lucy walks into the apartment. That's good. Cool breeze makes the paper on Carson's desk shudder and a bank statement, a notebook, a scattered pile of sticky notes lying between the desk surface and the windowsill. The computer window is open, too. Sometimes she drops in on him like this as he works from home, and today, how could she not? She has the best kind of news in her purse. It's positive news. But when she sees the woman's eyes paused in rapture on the computer monitor, she freezes. How could she not? It's not exactly like walking in on the act of infidelity and yet the pixelated form of it, all frozen in place while Carson takes a pee, is somehow just as bad of a gut punch. She expected to see Excel sheets, and at worst, YouTube home repair videos. No. He has this blonde and busty woman *paused* and waiting for him to return.

She takes the news out of her purse. A positive. Two *months* positive. She sets the news on the desk and backs away with a narrow brow, and the breeze turns into a momentary puff of force and puts some of the paper on the floor. She sinks into the hallway when he comes out and watches him stand over the desk and scratch his head as he picks up the test and frowns at its meaning for a good thirty seconds. Will he press play now? Should she wait and see? How could she not?

The door is open when she leaves.

Fox of the Forest

Mark sat down and wrote a letter that he wasn't sure he would ever deliver. Not many people wrote letters anymore, of course, so he hoped such an ancient and thoughtful medium might suggest the urgency of the matter at hand.

Dear Dean,

What are you doing, dude? Why spend all your money on OnlyFans and Fanduel? Why gawk at those lulling screens? No more daft consumption. Out with you, to open fields, to charities and orphanages, to the widow's apartment, to the church potluck!

What are you doing, sick and feeble society, turned in on yourself, as you float in a sea of avatars, engaged in your disembodied discourse, minds like downed hound dogs who have forever given up the hunt for the elusive gray fox of the forest? Let's get back to you, solitary man. What do you do all day? Who's there to initiate you? To hold your neck-bearded head up? I won't call you "incel." I'll even apologize for calling you "dude." Let's start over. I'll call you friend—no, brother; who told you, brother, that you have nothing to offer, nothing in the world to do?

I'll give you kick starter and just say right off the bat: None of that's true.

Much love,
Mark

He put down the fountain pen and winced. He crumpled the letter and hurled it into the bin by the desk. In its place, he picked up his cell phone and called Dean.

"Hey man," he said. "Lunch?"

Blue Church

When I can't sleep, I sometimes tell myself a story. Well, it's not quite a story, I guess. More like an image. It amounts to a picture of an old man topping a grassy hill and finding himself within a stone's throw of an old church, all blue in winter's shadow, but with people still going into it—men, women, children, everyone. Even in the cold, even though the church is ancient, with a holey roof, in they go like silver minnows swimming in a cave, the morning light crafting golden beams through the crevices.

I don't know who the old man is in this story, but it's always an open-ended question whether or not he'll walk down the hill and enter the church himself. I like to think that he does. Everyone else is, or so it looks like. Where's he been all these years? What's he looking for through those scaly gray eyes? And when the snow starts, and he knows it probably won't be any warmer in the church, will he opt for the closeness of company or stick to his solitary self?

The image can't be a story, though, because by the time the old man finally starts down the hill and when it starts to snow and when the last widow and orphan go through the church graveyard, walk through the ragged doors, and sit on the pews, I'm already asleep, dreaming dreams I'll forget by morning.

The Poet of Old Parts

My father seems to applaud the tools and other appendages that function only half as well as they're supposed to. Need I remind myself of the '97 Suburban, which friends likened to a tank, or the garden fenceposts made out of old playground parts, jangled together with wire and a prayer? He only ever asked for hoses for his birthday as if utility should always cancel out want. "Cheapskate," my brother joked.

"Frugal," I said. "He's a frugal man."

Perhaps I'll amend the first paragraph in retro and say that *creativity* might better describe Dad's ramshackle put-togethers. He didn't want his backyard to turn into a junkyard akin to so many rural homesteads and so sifted among metals like a poet going after verbal pearls, refusing the instant YouTube or Amazon fix. I don't know if I've taken after my father. Of course, I wonder this as I cruise down a narrow backroad highway in a 2000 Toyota Corolla, contemplating getting a flip phone, chewing at the bit for just a modicum of simplicity in my life. My father, I think, just wants a world that works and which doesn't work against him.

His garden, long guarded by fenceposts made of reinvigorated junk, translated into vermin-thwarting pillars, seems to grow every year.

The Golden Age Ever Recedes

The other day, a college student named Joe catapulted back to a feudal society in eastern Europe and worked among the destitute for an afternoon. Before that, he sat in a sociology class.

A lord of the land paired him with a dude called Mort, short for Mortuary, who spat black stuff into cans and scratched at a worm on his wrist. These were golden years for humanity; far as the eye could see, the plains extolled extravagance, plentitude, God's gracious bounty. And Joe, being just a sophomore, undecided as to his major, a bulbous two hundred pounds, had a time keeping up with Mort's scything. Swish, swish, spat, went old Mort without nary a grunt to suggest he noticed Joe's existence.

"Can you tell me where I am?"

"Not where, not why, not *who,* nor how come, see?" cried Mort through his armpit. "'Nuff talk from a weasel like you!"

"Well, okay."

Next thing Joe knew he was back in sociology class at the very back row, pencil tip snapped against the page, the instructor at the helm of the room swiping through some outdated theory on the chalkboard. Swiping like he held a scythe.

Shoulders

The woodshed was a scanty lean-to at the edge of the property and was ink-blue in the dusk when the youngest of the family walked across the yard with his hands in his pockets and sat on the old chopping block all crisscrossed with axe marks. He was seventeen and due to go to college the next morning, but he didn't want to go all of a sudden and made no big secret out of it at dinner. Where he sat, the sun mulled like a brazen quarter just above the trees and the cicadas chattered in the woods past the pasture. He plucked the axe from the stump and held it in his farmer-bred hands.

If he stayed another two months he might learn to love the work that made him who he was. But he must go off and learn and become his own man and start a new life for himself in some other part of the country and return to this little scratch of woods for summers and holidays. He sat on the block and let the axe rest against his knee. The chopped wood from last year still stacked all the way to the roof of the woodshed behind him like a mountain of dominoes that one can't be too careful about upsetting. And yet everything here was solid and eternal and almost holy. He picked up the axe again and closed his eyes so the deep hues of amber sunshine made him see constellations in his eyelids. When he opened them up his father walked down the slight hill to the barbed wire fence with hay on his shoulders. When he came back up he would see his son and talk with him.

The Dock

RECALL summer camp? The dock? Here. Close your eyes. Try to follow my lead:

Rain-covered canoes, upturned, sampled with mildew, lay by the old camp lake in the Indian Summer haze, still set up on the rack where we used to philosophize with feet plugged in the muck, tank tops grimed with sweat and sun. Cicadas roar, tree frogs chatter, you laugh and opine and riddle the water with your feet. We sit on the dock now as evening waxes with forest discourse and wanes with the signets of stars and fireflies. We tend to forget these days how baroque the world really is: Stuffed to its brim with fissures that science can't fully plumb.

We can't stay here and forever talk, though, or neglect the tin buildings above. We can, however, mix words with the water, and let 'em join the ripples, which ebb as sonar waves into space and make mirages against the far side of the bank.

Wait. Maybe we *can* stay here. Can we? Maybe we never left.

Boots

My cousin Judd got stuck in the mud on Saturday morning next to the cattleguard. Or so it seemed, mind you! A little bit of grassy hill, more like a lump, hid Judd belly down so all I could see from the living room window was a child in a cowboy hat with his head bowed, fists jerking up and down like he was trying to play hopscotch with copperheads.

Ah, Judd. Dear cousin Judd. He wishes in his heart of hearts that he was a real cowboy. Three whole years younger than me, gangly as an underfed beanstalk, fresh on our land from the suburbs, he liked to colonize the ranch during his occasional visits with Uncle Don and Aunt Cici, liked to think that because our last name is etched on the entryway above the cattleguard, that he lays equal claim to the empire. Hmm.

What was I supposed to do? Pull him out?

Dad I had work to do out back. We needed to put up new fence and put out hay. Later this afternoon, before it snowed, we had to deliver a calf in the barn. Did I have time for this? To check on poor cousin Judd?

I decided that no. I didn't. I was a man now and couldn't always be looking after kid cousins. Time to work. But before I could turn away and snicker, Cousin Judd, who Uncle Don sometimes called "Dud" (a little too far, maybe) ran up to the house in his mud-caked boots with a fat copperhead snake dripping with venom and blood. "I killed it with my cowboy boot!" he shouted. "My cowboy boot!"

Freight Train

"WHY don't people ride trains anymore?" said Hilde. She watched the freight train rumble a mile off in a series of colorful blocks, covered quite wondrously, she thought, with every potential genre of graffiti. Her brother, two years older and buried with actual interest in his geometry homework, replied, "They do. Just not so much in America. Here they use 'em to move coal and rocks."

"Coal and rocks."

She looked away and picked up her backpack, figuring she should get going on her history report, which was supposed to be about the invention of the automobile. The sun fell slant on her face, on her brother's open textbook, on the slow-moving train on the other side of the little river.

"Where's it going?" she said.

"Huh?"

"The train."

"Why do you want to know about trains all the sudden? It passes by here every day."

Hilde shrugged. "My report is about cars and stuff."

She got involved in her report. She learned about Henry Ford's assembly line, oversaturation, the industrial revolution, World War I, tanks, and plastic plane hoods. The old trains still crisscrossed the west, but Eisenhower's interstate agenda cancelled the old ways. She could still ride a train in Durango, Colorado or hop on the Am Trak. But when she looked out the window again an hour later, it was dusk, the town was shutting down, and the train was long gone. All that remained were a couple of kids, not far from her own age, tottering on the rails and laying down pennies as if they wanted to buy tickets to some far-off and impossible place.

She closed her book and waited for her parents' car to roll around the block.

Creeks

When they were kids, they needed no philosophy of creeks and hills. They didn't need to know *why* they swam and rolled. Sean and Hannah were neighbors back then and never thought about tying marriage knots. Now, they got up and brushed teeth and brushed past one another in the halls. She went downtown to work in a high rise. He sat at home and called people he didn't know on behalf of a product he didn't believe in.

So, yes. Now the question of purpose, of philosophy, of ultimate ends, flowed in their heads like creek water, rose in their spiritual periphery like sun-inflected hills. For Sean, the question "Why" roiled in his coffee-warmed gut every single morning. For Hannah, it spun with pigeons in the air, bounced like the cotton bells on women's coats in Central Park.

But they both stowed away such questions. Everyone did. They also tried to forget the creeks and the hills. Everyone must.

Easier that way. Harder that way. Like flowing with a current just to swim against it. Just not flowing for fun.

Diner Soup in Tucumcari

Tucumcari's Main Street is a relic of a bygone age, but the USA still likes to bat its eyes at the past. The town is a slow-pumping heart, the aorta valve gasps, but still: It lives. Stuart felt like he stepped into a roadside museum when he rolled into town on a Friday and chanced upon Frank's Drive-In Diner. The jazzy red sign, newly painted, crowned with Edison-style light bulbs, the Route 66 mural on its side, the memorial Ford Mustang on its lawn of pebbles by the parking lot, all bespoke old laughs and milkshakes and red lips and tucked in dress shirts. Interstate 40 roared a mile off. The wretched Interstate 40, killer of smalltown America, was like a snake bellied over its prey.

"What'll it be, champ?" asked the waiter across the counter.

"Uh. . .hey, chicken noodle soup sounds good, I guess," said Stuart.

"Well that *does* sound good. Smart choice."

Stuart smiled lightly, nodded. He liked the old couple in the corner booth. They stared through the window with their arms crossed, needling their wrinkled fingers, their white diner mugs filled with coffee. No one in there was from Tucumcari, though. Everyone was passing through. Vacation. Business. Onto the West. The young woman sitting on the sparkly red stool a few feet down might've been on a road trip to find herself. She wore a purple Patagonia fleece, a pair of wearied hiking boots, and her winsome eyes explored the diner with bemusement, maybe even desire for something she couldn't articulate. Maybe she was on mission to discover America—the real one. Had she found it? Had Stuart?

He ate his chicken noodle soup, thanked the nice man across the counter, and drove on.

Baptism

He sits on the edge of the spring that he and his neighbor found all those years ago and bows his head in his orange hoodie and those ridiculous camo pants he once thought would distinguish him in the garish high school halls. He has a real struggle articulating the strangeness of his life since it's now on the brink of real change. Nothing is even *over* yet; it's only *almost* over. Can he vault back to a world where society comes pre-constructed, the neighbors are ever nigh, the cat ever-licks his orange paw in the light of a June morning?

The spring is there, though. It's quiet and clear, and Cormac McCarthy's trout and their wimpling fins might speak of something than can't be made right, that can't be put back together, but that doesn't mean the spring isn't real, or shimmering, or reflective of some abiding, long-term truth, one that outlives lonely men. What does the spring *mean*? Symbolize? Reflect? Don't ask the boy as he sits on the spring's edge. Later he'll learn about rhetorical analysis and deep readings. Of meanings and interpretations. But not yet. His dad will find him out there, or maybe a brother, or maybe God, and one of them will tell him the truth—that "it," however elusive, whatever *it* is, isn't beyond reach, isn't gone.

Ten years later, *today*, he tries to remember whether anyone ever came to let him know that. Maybe he's got to go looking again, go back, go forward. Go in.

Question Mark

THE egret poses like an ivory question mark in the middle of the half-dry lake. The arid ridges of the banks tell of drought, of contracting territories, of shallower standing waters, offering statement, declaration: Leave for better water!

The egret is a praying shaman in the afternoon sunshine, though, instated like a fluid statue. Even in altered topography, cracked mud like earthy puzzle pieces making maps of peculiar design, the bird stands on a piece of old tree tacked to the muddy lake floor. Why are you so comfortable, egret, as though you believe the rains will flow tomorrow, restore the wasteland to harmony? The counterpoint question mark strikes with the rumble of distant thunder: How else, worried, watching human, am I supposed to live?

A PRODIGAL SON

HIS old church, its uptight community, smiling faces, rows and rows of nice men and nice women and a guilt-tripping pastor, khakis and pastel golf shirts—none of it swims in Terry's eyes as vividly as the colors of the night club a thousand miles away from that old childhood venue of judgment. Nothing can distract him now from the swaying bodies, high-raised glasses, the pulsing techno music, the deafening chatter of the four hundred voices. Nothing can replace the DJ in his loose T-shirt and pants that sort of look like ripped up khakis, who stands at the helm of the palace in his lectern of glory and beckons the worship of the congregants. Nothing can supersede his new beatific vision.

The beat drops and the ecstasy powers its way through the dim room, turns the world upside down, crowds him into a new set of parameters, promises him freedom from the world, from himself.

At the end, though, it's the same story. He wakes up in a bed by himself and rubs his head, the gray sunshine streaming through the window, borne of a mysterious source of light.

Monday, Already December

Monday, already December, winter raising its star, soft frost on the still-green grass, melded with copper carpets of leaves. This year is already close to conclusion, nearing a cold interim before the next fell swoop.

Monday, already December.

Never ready, am I, to sit in the winter stills, stock still, and listen to the cathedral bells, their tinny timbres and twangs, singing through these scarred timbers.

Monday, already December, year already seasoned, pressed, and layered like flour in a measuring cup. This year is an epilogue to a fast flinch, a muscle spasm, birthing out months of sadness, left to gather up on the frost-green ground, become an ornament, become a Child.

Monday, already December.

Acknowledgments

"A Dog Named Job" originally appeared in *Literally Stories.*

"The Dock" originally appeared in *Vilas Avenue.*

Thanks, as always, to the support of friends and family.

www.ingramcontent.com/pod-product-compliance
Lightning Source LLC
LaVergne TN
LVHW020646100826
845148LV00012B/2347

* 9 7 9 8 3 8 5 2 7 7 2 4 7 *